MACLEISH SQ.

MACLEISH SQ.

A NOVEL

DENNIS MUST

• • •

ILLUSTRATIONS

RUSS SPITKOVSKY

Red Hen Press | *Pasadena, CA*

Book design by Mark E. Cull

Library of Congress Cataloging-in-Publication Data

Names: Must, Dennis, author. | Spitkovsky, Russ, illustrator.
Title: MacLeish Sq.: a novel / Dennis Must ; illustrations, Russ Spitkovsky.
Other titles: MacLeish Square
Description: First edition. | Pasadena, CA: Red Hen Press, [2022]
Identifiers: LCCN 2022007379 (print) | LCCN 2022007380 (ebook) | ISBN
  9781636280592 (paperback) | ISBN 9781636280608 (ebook)
Subjects: LCGFT: Novels.
Classification: LCC PS3613.U845 M33 2022 (print) | LCC PS3613.U845
  (ebook) | DDC 813/.6—dc23/eng/20220224
LC record available at https://lccn.loc.gov/2022007379
LC ebook record available at https://lccn.loc.gov/2022007380

The National Endowment for the Arts, the Los Angeles County Arts Commission, the Ah-
manson Foundation, the Dwight Stuart Youth Fund, the Max Factor Family Foundation, the
Pasadena Tournament of Roses Foundation, the Pasadena Arts & Culture Commission and
the City of Pasadena Cultural Affairs Division, the City of Los Angeles Department of Cultural Affairs, the Audrey & Sydney Irmas Charitable Foundation, the Meta & George Rosen-
berg Foundation, the Albert and Elaine Borchard Foundation, the Adams Family Foundation,
Amazon Literary Partnership, the Sam Francis Foundation, and the Mara W. Breech Foundation partially support Red Hen Press.

First Edition
Published by Red Hen Press
www.redhen.org

For MBIW-J

Darl has gone to Jackson. They put him on the train, laughing, down the long car laughing, the heads turning like the heads of owls when he passed. "What are you laughing at?" I said.

"Yes yes yes yes yes."

—William Faulkner, *As I Lay Dying*

All men live enveloped in whale-lines. All are born with halters round their necks; but it is only when caught in the swift, sudden turn of death, that mortals realize the silent, subtle, ever-present perils of life. And if you be a philosopher, though seated in the whale-boat, you would not at heart feel one whit more of terror, than though seated before your evening fire with a poker, and not a harpoon, by your side.

—Herman Melville, *Moby-Dick*

MACLEISH SQ.

PRELUDE

I'm a painter. Well, I play one. It's why I came back to live in my hometown, the burg of three rivers, having resided on the fringed edges of the metropolis for most of my adulthood. But when I grew closer to the final trimester of life, bits of my boyhood began to reemerge out of the darkness of time. Events, places, and people I hadn't thought about in years rushed back like water seeping under a door. *What was this all about?* I wondered.

It was that period in time when I was truly happy.

Also, my earlier acquaintances, I realized, had begun living double lives. Once we were together, they'd feign a devil-may-care insouciance, "I live for each day," when in fact in the confines of their own foreshadowed rooms, they had begun to write their wills and compose their epitaphs. I envisioned each as pushing his gravestone backward and forward not unlike the hoarders and wasters in Dante's *Inferno*.

I was not about to succumb to the inevitable. I would be attired in burial weeds soon enough. Why should I take masochistic delight in accosting Mr. Death before our date at the River Styx?

Thus, approaching my seventieth year, I bought a small farmhouse on the outskirts of the now mostly desolate mill town where I'd grown up but fled when I was eighteen. Despite its dereliction, the burg was alive with old memories as if they had reached out to greet me. I'd enjoyed no such ambiance in the metropolis.

I couldn't walk down Main Street without recalling my old

haunts: the haberdashery now boarded up where I bought my first suit; the rococo movie theater, demolished for a parking lot, where I first encountered Stanley Kowalski and escaped my chrysalis that very night; the schoolhouse now converted to a tenancy where I—along with many of my friends—felt robbed of daylight and, if nothing else, had learned irony.

Even St. Mary's Church where I took confession with Father McCarthy had been razed. It was he who turned me and several other boys on to the *Inferno*, permitting our weekly sessions in the ecclesiastical phone booth to become a source of mirth. Upon uttering our confession, the jovial priest would inquire into what downward circle King Minos, the wretched long-tailed monster, should fling us. Most often it was Circle Seven: *Violence*. I was initially confused until my friend explained what Father told him: "You are violating the natural purpose of your penis." In penance for our sins, instead of having us repeat Hail Marys, the priest would quiz us on some intricacy of Hell, say, "Why are flatterers submerged in shit?"

We adored the man.

To this day I swear the rivers that run through our town are Acheron, Styx, and the rust-red Phlegethon, just as Father would have it. We swam in all three.

One day I happened to pass on the street the very woman I thought I would marry. Still, I'd no interest in speaking to her, for it was more enjoyable to be washed over by the recall of what once was . . . all too pungent, bittersweet, but nonetheless electric, alive.

So, for months I repaired and freshly painted the two-story clapboard house with squirrels in the attic. A large shed stood in the dooryard to which I decided to add several windows. I fancied the notion of having a private place, a light-filled retreat.

"Occupy the main house with ghosts!" I laughed to myself. "You need a place to escape to."

So many things in life—some might say most—make little sense. *I couldn't even draw.* Yet that afternoon I understood why I had returned to this place: all the memories bubbling up inside me, that young febrile past where each experience, having no precedent, would begin to find its expression on canvas.

Two years later, on a day analogous to that epiphany moment—except it was wintertime and the brilliant sun had turned the snow outside the studio's windows to crust—an inscrutable young man in a mackinaw jacket stood gazing in, his tousled hair the shade of straw.

When I stood, he disappeared.

I opened the studio door and cried out, "Hello?"

No response.

Once outside I spotted his tracks and followed them toward a glade of white birch a short distance away.

That's when we exchanged eye contact.

"What is it you want?"

He didn't answer. His hands were plunged into his jacket pockets, causing the threadbare fabric to pulse. The cloth sneakers were soaked.

"Come in," I said. "I'll make you some hot tea with lemon."

No response.

As I turned and walked back to the studio, the snow crunched behind me.

Inside, I sat him down and heated the water. He held the cup with both hands, barely raising it to his lips.

"You must be hungry."

He cast his eyes downward.

That morning I had made myself a sandwich and now unwrapped it for him. It was evident he hadn't eaten in some time. When he finished, I motioned that he remove his wet jacket and untie his shoes while handing him a blanket from my studio couch in which he wrapped himself.

I returned to my easel.

Perhaps for a whole hour no words were exchanged. At one point I heard him stir, and then sensed he was standing behind me.

"Who's the boy?" he asked, his voice a trifle hoarse.

I had been inspired by Matisse's *Piano Lesson*.

"Nobody in particular."

"The woman behind him?"

"Same."

"Do you live alone?"

"I do."

He pointed to the farmhouse.

"Yes. This is my studio where I go most days to paint. I'm rather fortunate, wouldn't you say?"

He nodded and sat back down.

I took a chair across from him.

"Now, please tell me why you are here. I don't believe you were just wandering by."

His steely gaze unsettled me.

"What's your name? Mine is—"

"I know who you are."

"*You do?* Well, most of my neighbors don't. It's one of the many reasons I delight in living here."

"You're John Proctor."

As if I were being accused.

"Is the name familiar to you?" I asked.

He nodded.

"So, what might I call you?"

"Eli."

"Eli who?"

"Just Eli."

"Fair enough," I said. "I'm finished here for the day. Let's head inside."

And that evening after a full dinner, where he ate enough for each of us a couple times over, Eli concisely explained how he'd come to find me. He'd been living in a New England community near the coast. As a child he'd stayed with his mother, but more often lived among friends when she was sent off to rehab between long bouts of intoxication.

"In the Lord's name, Eli, how did you end up here?"

"My grandmother."

I stared at him, bewildered.

"Told me she knew you."

I still wasn't getting it.

"Said you might take me in."

At that moment, the innocuous afternoon meeting of a bedraggled young man who had taken refuge among the white birch took an ominous turn.

"To live here?"

"Yes." His hands began rolling their fingers together.

Not wishing to hurt him in any way, I was reluctant to respond. "Do you drink coffee?"

He said he did.

After I poured each of us a cup, I sat closer to him. "Eli, let me explain something to you. I'm about to turn seventy. The Holy Bible says three score and ten is the normal life span. So, you might say I'm living on borrowed time, and the many decades I've left behind included no children as well as a marriage that lasted the length of a wedding candle. Which is to say so damn short the pain disheartened me from ever trying it again.

"In brief, I've made no lasting connections to anybody or anything my whole life. Not to say that I'm proud of it. I've settled down here outside the derelict mill town of my childhood to savor the days each sunup deigns to grant me."

I took a deep breath and reached to grab both his hands.

"Somebody is badly mistaken, boy. Surer than hell!"

"Sara Phipps," he muttered.

We locked eyes.

"Your grandmother?"

"Yes."

"She never remarried?"

"No."

"Eli—Christ be my witness—Sara Phipps vanished prior to our first anniversary. I'd no idea what I did or hadn't done that caused her to flee. But it must've been dreadful because it plagues me to this very day. Queered me, she did.

"Least she could have done was left a note alleging I had nothing to do with it."

I was still revisiting the pain of that early love affair when Eli spoke.

"Says she was with child when she left you, Mr. Proctor."

"Well, goddamnit, boy, *be she Mary or Semiramis!*"

I rose from the table, yanked open the oven door then slammed it shut. Eli sat staring out the back door.

I turned to him: "Why name me? I didn't leave her. I would have held on through thick and thin, health and sickness. But now shot out of the blue, *I'm in some way . . . a goddamned father?*"

"Is that what she told you?"

He nodded.

I burst out laughing.

"How could that be, son? You would be in your early forties! It just makes no goddamn sense."

Eli looked away. "Mother knows you."

It was as if a gust of arctic wind had blown open the studio door and robbed me of my breath.

The unspoken word combusted to life.

Without even attempting to address my former wife's iniquitous implication that I, John Proctor, had fathered a female offspring I never knew existed, I lashed out.

"Had her memory failed her in recalling any of her paramours? Oh, pick on John Proctor. Who wouldn't remember that name? Jesus H. Christ! Do you see what I'm trying to say, Eli? I know she's your grandmother and all, but . . ."

He shuffled over to where his shoes were drying and began lacing them up on his bare feet.

I plunked down on a kitchen chair, anguished that Eli believed I was his birth father and had once profaned his mother . . . my daughter.

With his coat now on, he headed for the door.

I grabbed him, turning him about. "It's got nothing to do with you. Or maybe even me. You asked who that boy seated at Matisse's piano was? I had no idea. Except now. Maybe you do, too."

And I pulled him to me, wet mackinaw and all.

"Up the stairs, the bathroom is to the right, your room is across the hall. Leave the shoes on the hot-air register. They'll be dry by morning. Hand me your jacket. I'll hang it close to the furnace in the basement.

In bed that night, I reflected on his and my conversation, wondering what Father McCarthy, if he were still alive, might have uttered in the confessional about Eli's mysterious arrival.

"God works in mysterious ways, John Proctor. Perhaps he is your son." I envisioned the ecclesiastical phone booth exploding with mirth.

Mercifully, we ceased mentioning Sara Phipps, or the mother he never named—with a sole exception: one evening he volunteered, "Mother had many men . . . none my father. I found my own way through each day."

Eli was a taciturn yet studious fellow who lost himself in reading from my ample collection of authors. And given that he especially enjoyed listening to the long-playing albums I had amassed of various jazz pianists, on a whim one day I bought him an aged Chickering upright from a Baptist church outside of town. To my delight, he was soon transcribing simple melodic lines from one of those recordings.

* * *

Several months later, he came into my room at 2:00 a.m., waking me from a sound sleep.

"What is it?" I switched on my bedside lamp. He looked frightened in a way that I have experienced myself a few times in life. An unearthly fear.

"Son, what's come over you?"

"I think I am going to die."

I had to suppress a grin. Why, it was as if he were a four-year-old, yet he was an insightful young man of ruddy complexion and ready wit.

"Eli, get a hold of yourself." I reached out and drew him alongside me to the bed. "Was it a bad dream?"

"He visited me tonight."

"Who?"

"My father."

I sat up.

"'Come back, boy,' he said. Standing at the foot of my bed, he asked me to return home. 'Get dressed and come back with me.'"

"Could you see him, Eli?"

"Yes. His face looked pale in the starlight coming from outside my window. He wore a white shirt with no tie, its sleeves rolled up beyond his elbows. He had on a pair of striped suit pants, and his ink-black hair was combed straight back, glistening like it was wet. He held out his hands, coaxing me to follow. What do you think this means?"

I was hesitant to answer. The visitation, stark as Eli had described it, prophesied the apparition's return. Or, worse, that Eli would be induced to follow.

"Am I going to die?"

"Not alone," I replied, forcing a smile. "From here on we'll share this bedroom together. You needn't be afraid."

But over the days that followed Eli's look confirmed he'd become preoccupied by the visit. This was a young man who loved books, but recently he stayed in his room staring out that window. We had often sat down to dinner together; now it was difficult to get him to the table. We did share my bedroom, but he'd sit up at the slightest of noises, certain his *father* had returned.

His mounting anxiety affected my work. The amity we'd enjoyed for all these months had been disrupted.

In a sense I, too, awaited the stranger's return.

* * *

He reappeared several times, in fact.

Always dressed in the same manner. Like all other nights: *"Come back, boy. Get dressed and come back home with me."*

Now that Eli slept in my room, I would shudder witnessing in the faint light his expression iced by abject fear as he stared at the figure at the foot of his bed.

"He's not real, Eli. There is no one except you and me in this room. Lie back down. It will all be fine in the morning."

Yet in my heart I knew it wouldn't be. The stranger had stolen the young man's will, his thirst for living, his omnivorous intellect. His beloved piano hadn't been touched in weeks.

It was only a matter of time. One day Eli would disappear.

For I, too, had been visited by a voice—first when I was startled in a senior English class by a derisive laughter erupting in my head followed by the accusation: "*Who are you kidding? None of this interests you. You know it . . . and so do I.*"

Called upon to answer a question in those moments, I stared blankly at the teacher. Classmates suppressed laughter as she chided me for daydreaming. And that evening, as I crossed one of several bridges in our town on my walk home from school, the voice returned. "*When are you going to find the courage to jump, John Proctor? Or will you always be the coward we both know you are?*"

Over two years it taunted me numerous times a day: to turn on the gas without lighting the stove when I was home alone, to swim out into one of the three rivers and never return to shore. Each day the voice intermittently gutted my will to live until I could withstand its malicious whispers no longer. Finally, I pled with it to grant me a week with no visitations so that I might experience each of those final seven days the way I once had. If the voice kept its promise . . . so would John Proctor.

"*Pick the river, sir. Choose the bridge from which you want me to leap . . . I will abide by your wishes. Then we'll see how real you are and what coward I am not.*"

But on the eighth day, he didn't show.

Why? I don't know. Yet there isn't a daybreak to which I awake and fear hearing: "*You must have thought I forgot about you, eh?*"

So, when Eli asked: "Am I going to die?"

I couldn't permit that for either of our sakes.

* * *

One late afternoon I caught him as he was about to leave.

"Eli, you are frightened, aren't you?" I sensed he was afraid the stranger in striped pants awaited him outside our door.

Earlier he would have ignored the query, assuring me he'd return soon.

He turned to face me. "How soon before I follow him when he says, '*Come home. Come back with me, Son.*'"

"Except he hasn't said *that* yet, has he?"

"What?"

"Called you '*Son.*'"

"No."

"Well, I do. I'm not about to let you go.

"Trust me, Eli."

He'd found his old mackinaw that I'd stored away in the attic. When I approached, asking him to hand it to me, I saw instead the disheveled young man who had watched me from outside my studio window. He had retreated into that feral persona to escape what he dreaded was shadowing him. That scourge wouldn't have registered to Eli then, for now he had something to lose.

As did I.

"Come," I said. "Sit alongside me. I want to know about your past."

"But why?"

"That apparition you describe in the white dress shirt, sleeves rolled up above the elbows and raven hair slicked back with no part—you must think who that may be. Perhaps he is a composite of several men, say, one of your mother's or Sara Phipps's lovers who guided you to my door. That person appearing at the foot of your bed has had to come from somewhere, son."

* * *

From our first meeting I believed there was much going on inside Eli's mind that he was loath to reveal. He was not about to disturb the conventionality—for want of a better word—that life with me afforded him. There were no surprises. He'd found someone who saw that he was provided for while affording him the freedom to consider matters other than getting through a day, surviving, leveling out the highs and lows.

Paradoxically, the routine gave rise to the existential threat he now experienced.

I surmised Eli had no real home for years, perhaps since he was as young as ten. He was suspect of my reaching out to him in a caring manner. He bristled at benign parental gestures.

The day I bought him a handsome wool peacoat, it hung for days in the downstairs closet, untouched. One night after dinner I insisted he try it on for me. Eli bristled and stood mannequin-like as I put it on him. "Look at yourself in the mirror!" I sang to no effect. Dispirited I hung it back up. One inclement Sunday afternoon a month or so later he came in from outside wearing it without either of us exchanging glances.

Or the Chickering acquisition that I thought might elicit a warm thanks, perhaps even a self-conscious embrace. But there was scarcely more than a niggardly nod of acknowledgment.

Yet that was enough for me.

Further, I had no real reason to attribute his being distant to my chafing over the implication of incest.

My guess was that his mother's place is where he returned for a brief period. That he'd found his way in a city environment where different friends would take him in from time to time. Eli, if nothing else, was resourceful, independent. Not once in the months that we'd been together had he reached out for me to assist him in any undertaking. Even when he initially watched me cook, I could detect a sly grin he attempted to mask.

How quaint, he must have mused.

The care with which I cleaned the house, or kept his clothes freshly washed and pressed, or bought him new clothes . . . registered as an amusing charade that he observed from afar. I even entertained the notion that Eli was amusing himself at my expense.

But as the weeks passed, it was as if the boy inside him was beckoned to emerge. He'd observe me in the studio, beguiled by how I would approach a blank canvas then over days an image would emerge . . . and by my ability to do more than slavishly copy a photograph or one of the white birches outside my studio window.

I'd witness him duplicate the process when he'd sit at the piano, sometimes for hours at a time. He'd compose in his own manner. Not that he'd studied music, but he had an excellent ear and knew harmony. I recognized the influence of specific jazz artists begin to manifest itself in his miniature compositions.

I continue to relish the afternoon he flawlessly performed Wynton Kelly's rendering of "Willow Weep for Me" on the upright whose strings over countless Sunday worship services had only thrummed to "Nearer My God to Me." And as I sat in the adjoining room listening to Eli perform, I rejoiced in the enigma of his sojourn. The young man carried his own light.

From that moment whenever I picked up a brush to resume painting, I couldn't help but contrast Eli's gift with my lack of one.

And then there was one early morning in the dead of our first winter that I spotted water seeping into the ceilings of the upstairs' rooms, especially his and my bedrooms. I quickly realized that ice dams had begun to form on the roof and summoned Eli to assist me in retrieving the wooden barn ladder that I stored outside my studio. We both bundled up and after positioning the ladder against the eaves, I took a hatchet and proceeded to climb the two stories.

After observing me timorously holding on while attempting to chip loose the ice dam for a couple minutes, Eli called up: "Can I try?"

He had evidently observed how wary I was of heights. In truth I tense up while crossing any bridge on foot or in a car. I dare never look down.

Back on the ground, I witnessed Eli scrambling up the spindly ladder to climb directly onto the glazed pitched roof, showing no concern that he might slide off. Within less than a half hour, as I watched, he relieved each of the dams that had formed. He then shoveled all the snow off the roof.

Once back down, he said: "John Proctor, no need to put the ladder away until spring. Wouldn't you say?"

"Oh, yes," I agreed.

Then he turned to me.

"I like helping out here."

No sly grin.

I cooked us a hot breakfast that morning. Eli built his first fire in the living room hearth.

Something between us had begun to feel real.

When he arrived, there was a dog-eared paperback of Melville's *Moby-Dick* in his jacket pocket. Each night he read in bed prior to falling asleep. Even when he shared my bedroom, his reading light remained illuminated long after I'd turned mine out. I, too, loved books and kept adding shelves to accommodate them. Eli lived in a library of sorts.

So, it was this one twilight when I'd beckoned him away from the front door, removed his jacket, and led him to the sofa where I sat alongside him.

"Tell me, Eli. I want to know who you were—perhaps even still are—before I welcomed you inside. I don't even know your last name. *Eli who?*"

CHAPTER ONE

I am Eli.

Of a thousand parts.

I hail from MacLeish Sq. overlooking a harbor north of Boston.

In the center of the square stands a bronze statue of Nathaniel Hawthorne that more closely resembles Rodin's famed rendering of Balzac, the one that some critics labeled "a sack of plaster, a block of salt left in the rain, a stalagmite." But those of us who call this place home see ourselves reflected in his disintegrating form.

After midnight when the Falling Man tavern closes, and the skylight is overcast, its patrons often caress the bronze casting as they traverse the square, tramping back to their places of rest. I've seen some even sing to the venerated author's defaced likeness, for it evokes their image of themselves. As if they, too, carry Naumkeag's stories within their souls yet have not put them to pen. Indeed, after owl light, the tavern becomes an audible manuscript in progress. But without fail the libations take hold and the anecdotist *du jour* loses his audience.

Immediately north is Charles Bridge, a replica of its namesake in Prague. It is a walking bridge and crosses the Acheron to the infamous Golgotha Hill where nineteen men and women were once executed, and another man, Giles Cory, was crushed to death. We refer to that other side of the bridge as the *invisible world*, or Netherland. A few of our regulars reside there.

Most, however, live in one of the modest domiciles off narrow

Hester Alley that commences at the square and runs directly east for several blocks to the harbor.

Our lives largely revolve about the Basilica, Falling Man Tavern, Cotton Mather Hotel, Naumkeag Library, a few stores, and the gathering areas in MacLeish Sq. itself. The Basilica alone defines us. There is no presiding clergy; aged women in gray homespun smocks are its guardians. After dark they designate its pews as sleeping quarters for the homeless. The night tenants—in return for these privileges—remove all their belongings and sweep out the Basilica at daylight. The guardians open its cathedral doors midmorning to the visiting pious, remnants of the defunct faiths. The disenfranchised use the pews—to which they have become accustomed—as their addresses, e.g.: "Goodman Brown–Aisle Three in the Nave."

The Basilica's interior is gutted of doctrinal embellishments save for the giant rood suspended in the apse. It is an iconic facsimile of the crucified Son of God but with toenails painted cerise. When the church doors close for the night, the Christ figure radiates a lime-green glow over the "parishioners." As a boy, when I first sought refuge in MacLeish Sq., I was permitted to sleep in the chancel, taking comfort in being illumined.

But the Basilica's nave verily comes alive from midafternoon until dark, when it becomes the Sq.'s community center. It's where we produce our plays, conduct dances, hold lectures, readings, and even permit those who are so moved to speak from the pulpit on Sunday mornings.

The Basilica is our mother in the same manner as the fragmented likeness of Hawthorne is our birth father.

* * *

At the base of Hester Alley, and directly across from the harbor, stands a red brick Federal style building with granite steps leading to an august portico and a fanlight entrance door. MacLeish Sq. residents refer to it as *La Porte d'Enfer*, despite it having once been the custom house. On a foggy night one can stroll down to the water and imagine a ghost ship on the horizon. People say they've seen shades leaving those ships and swear they are evacuees from one of the nine levels of Hell.

"Where else could we have come from?" they challenge skeptics.

A wooden golden eagle had once perched on the former custom house's portico. It had been replaced with the blind half-human, half-serpent, coal-black King Minos who relies on his sense of smell and touch to determine into which circle of Hell he will dispatch each sinner by his long tail. It is not unusual for a local when passing *La Porte d'Enfer* to glance up at the *connoisseur of sin* and gingerly make the Sign of the Cross.

Perhaps it is our elected names that distinguish us as MacLeish Sq. regulars. One never believes he or she belongs to the community until one of the respected elders christens us with an identity of their choosing. And it doesn't happen until several have studied our every move and eventually warmed to us.

For a full year I continued to be Eli, the name I had been given at birth. Having been endowed with a gift of being able to make others laugh, often at my own expense, I ingratiated myself with the denizens. Also, I was more than willing to do errands. "Oh, let me do that for you," I'd offer and run off to the store for victuals, fetch a book from the library, or even share the money I'd earned with one headed into the tavern. It was consoling to feel wanted, a feeling I hadn't experienced when living with my mother. She longed to be coveted; I was unable to satisfy that yearning.

One spring day I was summoned by a covey of elders to appear at the center of the square. It was daybreak, a time when many of them gathered on benches that circled Nathaniel's statue. They christened me Esau and celebrated the occasion with a steaming crock of lentil soup.

Except I wanted to remain Eli and told them I wished to remain who I knew I was. "Esau had a twin brother and a birthright. Eli does not. I was *born* in MacLeish Sq."

"Then may your name grow to be as revered as ours," Giles Cory declared, provoking every one of the gathered to robust huzzahs.

His namesake was the gentleman who, during the infamous witch trials, had been crushed to death on Golgotha Hill for refus-

ing to answer if he would be willing to be "tried by God and Jury."
They placed him between planks and incrementally added stones
to compel his answer. His final spoken words: "More weight."

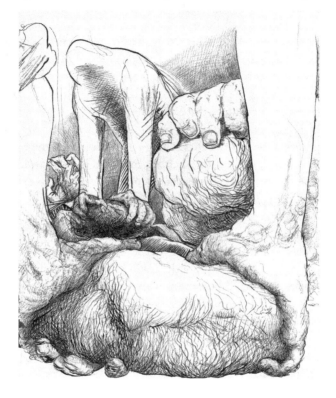

Giles was beloved by most every one of us, especially the men.
He'd rightly earned his sobriquet *More Weight*, for he was continu-
ally cuckolded by women. Several in the square had won his heart.
At the height of these affairs, he would embrace Hawthorne's enigmatic figure and sing, say, "I adore Francesca! Oh God, I'd even
perish for her." But within a fortnight word would get back to him
that she had been unfaithful, causing him to appear a shadow of
himself, a vague likeness. He'd wander the square in circles, often
gesturing to the author's semblance for an explanation, then piti-
fully shaking his head, knowing there wasn't any.

Heartbreak devoured the man. But then one day we'd see life spur his stride again. We began to become more manifestly cheerful ourselves. "Oh, Giles Cory, how wonderful to see you back to your former self. Thank God."

"No," he'd reply. "Thank Ariadne. I'm in love.

"More weight . . . please."

* * *

And who on a given evening could resist approaching Bartleby at his designated barstool in the Falling Man to request a favor, no matter how trivial, to delight in his *I would prefer not to* response? Unfailingly, a contagious laughter would begin to swell in the tavern, provoking Giles, the scrivener's soulmate, to rise and cast a baleful eye on the revelers and demand that chortling Dimmesdale "pronounce the first letter of the alphabet!"

Clapping would ensue. At this juncture all eyes would shift to the men's room door. An aggrieved bandy-legged inebriate would appear to point accusingly at the bartender and cry, "For the love of God, Montresor!" then disappear. A monastic silence would prevail, broken only by the sound of the bells trembling on Fortunato's jester's cap behind the lavatory's door. Laughter from the tavern's dark nook would bring yet another set piece rehearsed a thousand evenings to a close.

Pearl, a mute young woman attired in black crinoline, sat there knitting from a ball of red yarn the letter A, until she had a handful of them. These she would peddle in the square like flowers.

Having collapsed into an eerie reserve as if overcome by the jocular orgy, the tavern regulars now stared into their drinks.

As I grew older, I came to wonder if the denizens of MacLeish Sq. were actually phantoms reenacting their christened lives on earth. Had each come to this locale with its celebrated past seeking a storied identity? How else to explain the harbor sighting of a ghostly armada on the vanishing line?

Several men in the square who had been christened Ishmael had committed to memory the entire text of *Moby-Dick; Or, The*

Whale. Once each year, generally in the dead of winter, they would preside for an entire evening in the Falling Man, exchanging esoteric allusions to the text with brilliance and wit, eliciting boisterous applause and shouts from the gathered. These men were endowed with a tragic dignity that had escaped the rest of us. They were the square's holy men in robes redeemed by Herman Melville's words, a Queequeg[1] coffin amulet about each person's neck. They fraternized with no one, not even with each other.

It was not uncustomary to see one of them at night in evident madcap colloquy with Hawthorne's bronze.

* * *

John Proctor *did* take me in.

For several harmonious months we shared life together. I once swore to him, "Even if I learn who my birth father is, you will always be the real one."

Maybe our relationship could have continued forever; I had no reason to leave, to return to the square. Until a voice claiming to be my father insisted I return home.

Except I'd never known one.

The voice would interrupt my thoughts at any hour of the day or awaken me at night, turning merciless over time. To the point that when it wasn't speaking to me, I felt terrorized that it would.

I read in John Proctor's face fear as to where I was being summoned.

In MacLeish Sq. we called it Hester Alley.

Those who walked down that narrow cobblestone way alone late at night were seldom seen again.

"And who will you be meeting down Hester Alley after midnight?" was a common gallows-humor question to a tavern friend. Superstition warned about wandering the alley at that late hour.

---

1 Queequeg, the son of a South Sea chieftain who left home to explore the world, and the first principal character encountered by *Moby-Dick*'s narrator, Ishmael. When the *Pequod* sinks, Queequeg's coffin becomes Ishmael's life-buoy.

One tale had it that even if you had nary a thought of dying, one who did would clutch your arm and drag you with him down to the harbor where those luminous craft on the horizon line dropped off and picked up.

New faces were always converging upon MacLeish Sq.

Seldom would a daybreak occur when one taking a stroll through the square wouldn't spy a stranger gazing at the statue. Fresh blood replenishing our community, having wandered up from the harbor.

Yet I was being called home.

Up to that point in my young life I had only listened to the dictates of my own voice. Now there were two.

Ironic, in that when I resided in the square, I had no fears . . . and no father. Now that I was learning to feel affection for one, I was being summoned.

It is when I was about to surrender to the voice, John Proctor sat across from me that late afternoon and said, "Tell me, Eli. I want to know who you were, or perhaps even still are, before I welcomed you inside. I don't even know your last name. *Eli who?*"

"Eli," I replied.

And described for him many of those who lived in and around MacLeish Sq., a Babel of sorts. There were those who had been christened by the Ishmaels, having established their identities in the regional scribblers' works. They had been graced with immortality and carried themselves as such. Fragments of narratives consorting with each other, they were the familiar ones. Each seemed to delight in the other's good fortune.

But then there were the *others*. So called due to an air of anxiety they displayed, existing in the hope of being named. Each had his or her own story but feared being doomed to wander about MacLeish Sq. for a lifetime without being christened a recognizable identity. They were an agitated lot reflecting a humiliated expression as if guilty for not having been chosen. But approached by anyone in the square— one of their kind or the storied—each would compulsively recite their tale and importune the listener to share it with an Ishmael.

These souls were the MacLeish mendicants of which there were legion.

With rare exception they sat among themselves in the Falling Man at a table in its shadowy regions while pining to occupy a stool in the company of, say, Doctor Chillingworth or his ilk[2]. While the Basilica's nave most weeknights accommodated a catholic gathering that was more representative of the give and take that occurred during the daylight hours in the square itself.

Yet there existed a prominent group who conversed in arcane allusions to Dante's *Inferno*. Occasional nights they staged enactments of, say, the middle ring of the Seventh Circle, wherein the Suicides performed as trees and brush while being ravaged by the Harpies.

Even so, the Basilica was more hospitable to the no-names, for inside, many of them found sleeping quarters among the pews. The ladies in gray smocks, the caretakers, treated everyone deferentially, not only the august Ishmaels.

* * *

I told John Proctor about a man whose friends mockingly called him Fubar. He'd been a longtime resident of the square and it was evident to each of us that he would never be anybody other than who he was.

My first encounter with him came about on an early Saturday afternoon in the Square when several *others* had already gathered. Each tried to keep a half dozen feet between themselves to protect their arena in the hope that an audience would converge about them once they began to speak.

When Fubar appeared, he wore a white dress shirt with long collar points, a black wool tie, and a tweed blazer. His trousers and shoes were less formal. He made no attempt to establish eye contact and, as if auditioning for a part, perfunctorily held out his

---

2 Roger Chillingworth, the vengeful physician husband of Hester Prynne, protagonist of Nathaniel Hawthorne's *The Scarlet Letter*.

hand to us for the passage he was to read. Muttering to himself, he shrugged his shoulders and began to gesticulate and cry out:

"*RELEASE! RELEASE!*"

Again, and again.

"*RELEASE! RELEASE!*"

As if by summoning all his energy, calling upon his powers of transforming himself into yet another character—one of the countless in which he had played about the Sq.—Fubar, before our very eyes, was conjuring a ritual to take flight out of his mouth.

He willed to accompany his breath is the only way I can describe the scene I witnessed that afternoon. He'd suspended all irony and disbelief and had begun taking long breaths, when he sang:

"*Reeeelllleeeaaasssee!*"

Fubar had begun to fitfully leap while flailing his arms as if they were accomplices to propel his escape. Yet his body kept drawing itself back to the stage floor as he willfully tried to shake it off.

"*Please. For Chrissake, let me go.*"

Then, toward the close of this ritual—what else could I name it?—his dying cry of *release* was now little more than a heavy smoker's wheeze. Fubar never once looked up, wandering off into the shadows as before.

CHAPTER TWO

JOHN PROCTOR

MacLeish Sq.: was there such a place?

And if so, why did Eli's description so closely parallel what had befallen Jeremiah, my deceased brother?

It was as if his double had wandered up Hester Alley to elude the infinity that shadows each of us.

I couldn't help but conflate the Fubar tale with the day Jeremiah ran across the dry meadow in flames while dogged by a fiery scar. His arms whirling propeller-like and with a fixed ironic grin aroused by the travesty forming somewhere in his addled mind. He thought he could fly, unlike the rest of us anchored to the soil by our fears, our cowardice, our willingness to accept banality and constancy in exchange for the high caused by running alongside death.

It was Jeremiah's unspoken belief that the only way one could squeeze the most out of life was by testing its denial at every opportunity. To embrace life, you had to embrace death also . . . not fear it.

Of course, he knew that I did, and he found this a never-ending source of amusement and ridicule.

I also wondered how Eli, reading portions of it, was able to relate a convincing expository recall of MacLeish Sq. and its inhabitants. I delighted in his narrative's literary allusions and assumed that he had added them to entertain me. Initially I didn't doubt that such a place existed. That, indeed, it's where he had found refuge and spent most of his young life before seeking me out. After all, I stepped outside realism when I painted. Why couldn't Eli do the same?

But the young man was not seeking my approval when he recited. Neither did he await my response at the conclusion of his recall.

"Goodnight," he said and wandered off to bed.

That evening I lingered downstairs.

I wondered if Eli's preoccupation with the "father" summoning him home had anything to do with this MacLeish Sq. tale.

Should I encourage him?

Yet Hester Alley and the Falling Man tavern had begun to take on a life of their own in my imagination. The allegorical way he'd composed the Naumkeag locale in his mind . . . is that what enabled him to endure his early years living there mostly on his own? Was it his "book"? The ledger in which he wrote each day what he hoped, imagined, would occur? Were I to journey to his so-named mythical place, I would surely confront a pedestrian city square that bore scant resemblance to his.

I had no choice but to cajole the young man into not "returning home."

As I lay in bed that night, I envisioned *others* lumbering up Hester Alley, souls burdened with the yearning to escape private infernos. As if Eli were foreshadowing those who lay off the Atlantic's horizon line, awaiting to step onshore.

* * *

Unable to fall asleep, I could hear him tossing and turning in his bed adjacent to the outside wall. Moonlight cast an amber glow over his bed.

"Are you awake?" I asked.

"Yes."

"The Ishmaels. Did they always hold court in the square, and once it became dark, did they go their separate ways?"

"Several lived in the Basilica."

"Among the itinerants in the pews?"

"No. In the side chapels. Unlike all the other nightly residents, come daybreak the Ishmaels were not evicted by the ladies in gray smocks. A few had a band of disciples who shadowed them. It was not uncommon to walk down a Basilica aisle and hear an Ishmael tutoring one on the book's passages:

"*Father Maple preaches that Jonah is most grateful for God's punishment and abstains, clamoring to be released from the belly of the whale. Why?*'

"Each side chapel had a gate enclosure upon which the hallowed man would hang his black robe and the Queequeg coffin amulet."

"Eli, who do you think these men were?"

"I don't understand."

I sat up in bed. He was gazing at the ceiling, head resting on his hands.

"What do you imagine they did prior to entering MacLeish Sq.? They must have had some identity. You call them 'hallowed men.' But everyone has a past of some sort."

"Then what is mine?"

He sat up, staring at me.

"It's why I ask."

"Mine is all those voices in the square who each had a story . . . except the Ishmaels kept theirs to themselves. That's why we gave them a wide berth. They had no compulsion to recite theirs. I entered having none. Now I have legion."

In myriad ways the young man seemed more worldly wise than I. A "thinker" striving to use his intelligence among those who have lost the capacity to reason. From what little I now had gathered about his MacLeish Sq., I perceived Eli had become victim to its inhabitants' "rosary of despair."

I wanted to change the subject. "Eli, tell me about its hotel."

"Alongside a grassy common two blocks off the square."

"Will you describe it for me?"

"The Cotton Mather, a dowdy establishment whose lobby revealed a longing for a funereal past, replete with potted palms minus cuspidors as well as overstuffed chintz sofas and chairs missing their antimacassars. It had a curtained-off formal banquet dining room on its main floor that several of us would occasionally peer into for a source of amusement."

Eli chuckled to himself.

"Please explain."

"Well, it was often sparsely occupied except for an aging gentleman—who we christened Charon—decked out in a tuxedo with glossy lapels and red socks. While he sat at a grand piano playing Cole Porter tunes, off to the side stood a uniformed maître d' at attention. There was nary a soul at any of its tables set with bone china, silverware, and crystal glasses.

"It was quietly referred to as the *Souls of the Dead Dining Room.* Yet, at random times of the year, I or others from the square could peer through the sheer curtains and observe all the tables occupied by Cotton Mather and other principals of the witch trials engaged in robust conversation and conviviality . . . despite an uninhabited dining room the hotel patrons would witness instead.

"It was not unusual once owl light occurred for someone to suggest we head off to Mather's to see what was playing. Generally, it was only Charon tinkling 'Every Time We Say Goodbye.'"

Each of us laughed, for it was one of the favorites Eli would sing while accompanying himself on the Chickering.

* * *

Following that after-dark exchange, by mutual consent he and I fell into a pattern of heading off to the shared bedroom not long after dinner. For my part I had become enamored of Eli's MacLeish Sq. tale. *Was it stream of consciousness, or had he composed it in his head prior to sharing it with me?* By this time, I was convinced that he'd embellished much of what I heard, yet I wasn't certain that if perchance I visited such a place—his square at the head of Naumkeag's Hester Alley—I wouldn't be able to recognize its various residents.

I had a disquieting sense that something else was going on between us. Eli displayed a knowing awareness that belied his years. My affection for him was growing, yet at times I suspected he knew something about me that I had either forgotten or was not privy to.

So, while I laughed at some things he said, that laughter was always a tad guarded.

I had been an omnivorous reader over the years; each of the rooms in the house had shelves of books testifying to this truth. Part of my delight in listening to Eli relate his experience was his sly wit, referencing many of the authors I once favored. After several Mac-Leish Sq. installments, I knew for certain that he was obtaining much of his material from *my* personal collection, including those journals containing stories I'd penned decades earlier. Even so, I wasn't about to call him on it. One, I didn't want him to leave and succumb to the voice that so unsettled us both, and two, my life had begun to take on distinct meaning once again.

I intuited that Eli was in singular touch with himself, a quality I lacked but had not missed until he showed up that day.

And what was in it for this young man who, in many respects, was still a boy?

I couldn't say for certain, except that if I wasn't there to elicit from him the MacLeish Sq. narrative, one day he would disappear. I was, for the present at least, his raison d'être, permitting his Sundays to fold into Mondays. His troubled nights to daybreaks.

There wasn't a shared glance that failed to acknowledge this truth.

* * *

One night Eli sat up in bed and read from a journal about a former Jesuit monk.

> One Sunday morning a Frenchman ascended the platform in MacLeish Sq. with a mystical air. He had deep-set eyes and a head of snow-white ungroomed hair and opened with a brief prayer.
>
> "Open These Naive Minds, Oh Lord. Amen."
>
> For long moments he stared out across those of us in assembly. Some lowered their heads. I did not.
>
> "My white hair . . ." he explained, "when the Nazis occupied France,

I was arrested in the streets of Vichy. My hair then was shiny and black like their boots. At a brief interrogation before the SS tribunal, I protested I was ministering to the poor. They were unimpressed, insisting I was French underground, and ordered my captors to take me out into the alleyway.

"They drew my hands behind me, binding them to a telephone pole. I requested a cigarette. The commanding officer lifted one out of a pack in my cassock, placed it in my mouth. Five puffs later, he gave the order to ready the execution. The soldiers about-faced, clicked their heels smartly, walked ten paces, turned, then ceremoniously lifted their pistols to aim at a paper doily their commandant had pinned over my heart. The officer gave an assenting nod.

"They would count to three.

"I witnessed my life ruthlessly sped up so that I was unable to reflect on any of its cascading images as I awaited the crack of their lugers.

"I shut my eyes briefly after *zwei*.

"At *drei* I heard *HALT*!

"*Why the reprieve?* I thought . . . it would come any second now.

"Then I opened my eyes. A wizened ferryman, his anthracite eyes a hair's breadth away staring fiercely at me, held out his arms. 'I am a leper,' he said. 'Dare you embrace me? I will ferry you across this treacherous stream.' And as the two of us stood wavering in a peapod skiff, I drew him to my body and kissed his mouth.

"'What's wrong!' the commander shouted.

"'I don't know,' one soldier answered.

"'Somebody moved in front of him,' responded the other.

"'What do you mean? Shoot him!' the officer spat.

"'Perhaps he's what he says,' objected the first soldier.

"'Look at his hair!' exclaimed the second.

"The commander, now highly agitated, strode over to me. Brusquely he cracked his leather crop across my face and spat onto my vestments, shouting, 'This righteous fool cannot be the one we're after. He is old, his hair is white. The Jew-priest was a young man, cocky. We are mistaken.'"

And the old Jesuit thrust his unruly shock of egret hair, feathery and silken, out over the square's makeshift podium:

    "A simple, ignorant monk housed for moments the leprous body of Christ," he sang, "and the Nazis were cowed by His presence. An old man with white hair even they would have shot. *But the Holy Father?*
    "Satan blinked."

After several minutes, with the only sound in our room the dripping bathroom sink across our hallway, he turned to me:
    "Did you believe him?"
    "Who but Christ could the leprous ferryman possibly be?" I replied.
    Years earlier I had heard the former monk speak in the early days of my matriculation at a divinity school. Emile Dubois, a Jesuit who'd abandoned the Roman Catholic church in the tradition of Luther, had joined the seminary's Protestant theologians. Yet within weeks, my hope that there would be several others like him to guide me in my spiritual quest was crushed. The remaining faculty were not light of spirit as he but stooped by ecclesiastical laws and decrees.
    Dubois's goat-leather-tome colleagues breathed a sigh of relief when he flew back to Europe. The heretic was gone.
    After the monk's leaving, I thought, *I am alone and without inspiration.*
    "Is that when God died for you?" Eli asked.
    "As a young man I believed I had been called by the Lord to serve. It was at divinity school where I began to discover that it all had been a fabrication. Mine. And others who'd meant well."
    "*The wizened ferryman? If he wandered up Hester Alley, would you recognize him?*"
    "Yes," I said.
    It was in that moment I recalled Eli recounting his MacLeish Sq. boyhood sleeping quarters:

The Basilica's interior is gutted of doctrinal embellishments save for the giant rood suspended in the apse. It is an iconic facsimile of the crucified Son of God but whose toenails have been painted cerise. When the church doors are closed for the night, the Christ figure radiates a lime-green glow

over the parishioners. As a boy, when I first sought refuge in MacLeish Sq.,
I was permitted to sleep in the chancel, taking comfort in being illumined.

How could young Eli, alone and with no parental guidance, not have felt solace by the chancel's incandescent Christ looking over him while he slept?

Surely, by reading my story of the French priest aloud, he was seeking some affirmation from me that the light of the "wizened ferryman" still flickered.

My affirmative response help bond Eli and me. How, I am unable to explain. Except I now knew why he had chosen those passages from my journal. He was as fearful as I to be summoned home.

His breathing had softened.

I envisioned his Ishmaels in their black cloaks taking the afternoon sun in MacLeish Sq.

CHAPTER THREE
JOHN PROCTOR

There were perhaps all of two weeks when I barely spoke with Eli, who spent his waking hours confined to his room, surrounded by a stack of books and several journals from my shelves.

Even the nightly narratives had ceased. Once the lights were out, I'd wait for him to begin speaking, yet refrain from commenting when he didn't . . . until late one afternoon when he came to me and asked to read something.

"Something I wrote. The Ishmaels. You asked, 'Who were they?'"

"Do you honestly know?" I joked.

"There was a superstition about crossing the Charles Bridge to its other side," he replied. "Some believed that's where the Cotton and Increase Mather ghosts resided. The ones we witnessed at the hotel dining room. A forbidding place. But I had no such fear. Walking towards the ocean inlet, I came upon a small eatery.

"'Stove Boat'[3]—a hand-lettered sign in its window read.

"Inside stood a counter with a half dozen stools and a long communal eating table with abandoned church pews for seating.

"The place was unoccupied except for the cook.

"Chowder, the offering of the day. Cod or clam.

"I ordered clam and when the cook placed a bowl before me,

---

3 Stove Boat: "And what do ye next, men?" "Lower away, and after him!" "And what tune is it ye pull to, men?" "A dead whale or a stove boat!" *Moby-Dick*, Ch. 36.

I thought he looked familiar. He feigned no recognition of me, however.

"When it came time to pay, he spoke.

"'You're an intrepid soul to cross over Charles Bridge.'

"Then I recognized him as one of the Ishmaels.

"'I've found a home in both places,' he offered. 'We are more complex than nature appears to permit.'

"Later that week I visited him in his side altar and requested he begin tutoring me. In his capacity as a Basilica Ishmael, neither of us referred to his identity across Charles Bridge. Periodically I'd return to the Stove Boat and converse with him as if he were a different person.

"On one of those occasions he shared this story.

"It's called 'Eddy's Asleep.'"

* * *

By the end of the week, he'd be hungry. The New York Post classifieds gave him no satisfaction.

Uniformed Bell Telephone women clerks herded the applicants into a room the size of the Forty-Second Street library's reading room. Hart sat down at the table—ten men on either side—and was handed a packet of papers, requesting the standard information: education and work history.

A bespectacled, round-faced applicant eyed him from across the table. Hart couldn't understand the nature of the man's mincing smile. Returning to his task, he heard a whispered threat couched in base profanity and shot his head up only to encounter the character grinning ingratiatingly at him.

Hart now became nervous. Each time he returned to the application, the character ratcheted up his invectives. Cutting Hart with a razor blade in the bathtub while the tormentor performed fellatio. He'd copulate Hart with a Colt .45 while micturating into his mouth. Each time Hart raised his head, the screed ceased, and the man resumed that unnerving affectation of his, as if to say, "It ain't me you're hearing say that nasty stuff, buddy. Funny, though?"

Hart summoned the attendant.

"Wait until this is over, cocksucker," the maleficent character hissed. "I'll follow you home and stick it down your throat while pinching Voltaire's nose, you yellow bastard!"

Whereupon Hart shot up from the table, pressed the completed application into the attendant's hand, and, bypassing the elevator, loped down six flights of steps. On the street he sought refuge in a coffee shop, monitoring the plate glass window while huddled in a back booth. Minutes later, the sadist reappeared . . . his face obscenely mashed against the window, squinting. Unable to see Hart, he appeared grievously hurt and wandered off.

The guy could ruin my life in a small town. What are the chances of my ever seeing him again? But food is running out. Money or one week's rooming-house rent. Car fare for one week. Then the first pint of blood to sell. Ah, what's this?

WHITE CASTLE HIRING, ALL SHIFTS. WE TRAIN.

The following day (still no call from Bell), Hart stepped out of the elevator onto the twenty-seventh floor of a flat-iron building in the thirties. Small offices on either side of the narrow hallway were occupied by lone accountants, lawyers, insurance salesmen, detectives, literary agents—all behind varnished oaken portals with translucent glass panes identifying the occupants in inelegant black letters. Room 143 read "E. A. Tully, Esq."

Was this somebody's idea of a joke?

A middle-aged woman wearing a cameo broach at her alabaster neck gestured for him to take a seat. Her dress made her look like a character in an Egon Schiele poster.

"I did inquire if you have a prison record, didn't I, Mr. Hart?"

"Yes."

"And you said . . ."

"I have not."

"Mr. Tully will see you now, sir. Go through that door, please."

A tall, Black gentleman with a snowy beard and penetrating blue eyes stood fully attired in a chef's costume and a toque inscribed

"Big Whitey." Chromium counter stools with red leather seats abutted a Formica counter on which sat a glass case of freshly baked peach, raisin, lemon meringue, and apple pies. Mr. Tully assumed his post behind the counter in front of the large grill, blue and yellow gas jets illuminating its undersides. An orange drink bubbler sat at the far end of the counter, gurgling. Posters of Big Whitey hamburgers being devoured by cartoon men and women adorned the pale-green windowless walls, and the coin-operated, chromium jukebox selector attached to the counter sat blank except for Charlie Parker's "Repetition."

"Mr. Hart, slip into this uniform, please."

Tully handed Hart a pair of striped pants, a freshly laundered white shirt, a black leather bow tie, an apron, and a toque.

"Call me 'Professor,'" Tully joked, as he made the first hamburger, then had Hart slavishly copy him.

"All Whiteys, big or small, are prepared with finely chopped onions whether the customer wants them or not. It's why they taste so damn good." Tully rolled the ground meat in his thick hands as if it were fresh snow, then he'd slap it flat. Each time another burger was fried, it was tossed into the trash. Soon, he began cracking eggs with the one-hand method. First, a smart thrust to a hard surface, then with index finger and thumb, while the hand swooped to the skillet, the yolk and albumen were released unmarried. Again and again, Hart cracked the eggs against the skillet, arm lifted aloft as if he were a pianist then authoritatively down, dropping the unbroken yolks into the melting a slab of butter—*Banjo Eyes*.

"By spooning the hot butter over the yolks until they whiten, barely, you make *Eddy's Asleep*." Tully taught as if he were a maestro of dance.

"It's all in the wrists. Showmanship. Your customers watching your every move." Tully was a stickler for neatness, too. "This is no science, Hart. It's kid stuff. You're Big Whitey, remember. Now, onto *Mulligan's Jewels*."

Hart had no idea how long he and the "professor" had been at the grill with the absence of daylight to indicate the passage of time. He presumed it must have been four or five hours. Finally, the mentor removed his apron and toque and took a seat at the counter, opened a menu, looked up at Hart, and ordered lunch.

"Two *Big Whiteys* with *Ivories*, a side of *Mulligan's Jewels*, *Frank Capras* for my wife (he didn't have one), and one *Ménage à Trois*. Oh, and a slice of *Uncle Whiskers*. Light on the *Moo* in our *Wake-ups*, please."

Nonplussed, Hart stared at Tully. But went immediately to work, struggling to recall Tully's invented jargon for the various plates on the menu. ("Remember, you're in the entertainment business.") And despite his forgetting a step or two, got it all right except the splats. They were a little doughy in their centers. Tully sloughed it off.

"The wife won't eat them all anyway." He laughed and swept all the prepared food into the rubbish bin.

"Now you sit, Mr. Buddy. You must be hungry."

Jesus, is this God behind the counter?

He ordered the same as the professor, except he passed on the flapjacks and omelet but wanted ice cream on his apple pie.

"I'll get those dance steps down cold, Mr. Tully, don't worry."

"Oh, I'm sure you will. There's one more very important thing I want to tell you, son."

"What's that, sir?"

"You're no longer Buddy Hart."

Hart looked at him, puzzled.

"Whitey . . . always Big Whitey. We come in two sizes—Whiteys and Big Whiteys." (The Whiteys were a quarter and the Big Whiteys thirty-five cents, forty cents with cheese or "ivories.") "When the customer says, 'I want a Whitey,' you respond, 'Big Whitey, sir?' And when they say they want a hamburger, you say, 'One Big Whitey on the Fry!'

"You get it?"

"Yessir," said Hart. He liked this kindly professor. This was a bona fide hamburger school. And when he finished eating, Tully disappeared for several minutes, returning with a diploma that had a black satin ribbon attached.

Buddy Hart, this 17th day of November 1961, successfully graduated from White Castle Hamburger Institute. Signed, E. A. Tully, Director.

"When do I go to work, sir?"

"This evening, 125th Street, eleven-to-seven shift. They'll be having you bubble dancing 'n' working the counter for a day or two, then you'll be on the flames."

"Am I a short order cook?"

"Yeah, that's what you are, son."

"One more question, sir."

"What is it, Hart?"

"Would you have hired me if I had a record?"

"What'd you do, boy?"

"Nothing. But suppose I had?"

"Big Whiteys got no past. When I slid your Frank Capras into the trash barrel, so went Buddy Hart. You're Big Whitey now. To me 'n' anybody else from here on out on the opposite side of the counter. *You've just been saved, son.*"

* * *

His first night's work, Hart washed dishes when he wasn't waiting the counter. The 11:00 p.m. to 2:00 a.m. spell saw nonstop traffic. 3:00 to 5:00 a.m.—maybe a dozen customers in all. None of the staff spoke to Hart other than to issue orders. At five thirty, the establishment was overflowing.

"Two *Wake-ups* to go, light on the Moo!"

"One *Big Honkey* with!"

"*Humpty Dumptys* with toast."

"*Fruit Cakes!*"

Tully's colorful substitutes stayed in the twenty-seventh floor two-room suite. Each site had its own lingo. At no time this first evening did anyone call him Big Whitey.

One week passed at various sites: two nights at 125th Street, one at Fifty-Seventh Street on the west side, three in Jackson Heights (there they called him "Bernie"). Each shift Hart mostly cleaned and did janitorial work, only occasionally getting behind the counter. But he was no longer hungry and the anxiety about having to pay his rent eased.

His second week of work began at the end of the Van Cortlandt Park subway line. A White Castle stood alongside two Irish bars. Hart was summoned to work the grill from midnight to 8:00 a.m.

He'd fallen into a pleasant rhythm after several shifts at the same location. Regulars were beginning to refer to him as Whitey. Occasionally an inebriated customer would call out Big Whitey as a taunt. And his expertise at the grill was becoming more refined, his technique polished. (*"Remember, son, first you're an entertainer."*)

Hart found extreme gratification in a job well done. A short order cook, albeit with a limited repertoire. During the slow period he and the counterman might converse, but mostly he fed the Wurlitzer, having bribed the vendor to place the same recordings he had at the 125th Street location in his 244th Street stop.

"The Micks will have your balls, Whitey."

"Maybe we'll educate the bastards," Hart insisted.

Billie Holiday, Dexter Gordon, The Prez, Bird, Jimmy Lunceford's band, Monk, Duke, Ella, Dizzy, Bud Powell . . .

The second month, sometime after 2:00 a.m., Hart stood leaning against the counter, his back turned to the stools, staring out at the traffic on Broadway and listening to his tunes, when a stranger entered, sat down at the far end of the counter, and slid a menu out of its chromium grip. Hart's counterman had retired to the restroom with the Daily News.

"What will it be, sir?"

"I'm thinking. Give me a coffee."

"Cream and sugar?"

"Neither."

"Yessir. One *Wake-up* coming right up." *Jesus, the guy looks familiar. Where in hell have I seen him before?* "Anything else?"

The customer didn't lift his head. "One poached egg on toast."

"*Sally Takes a Bath on the Square!*" Hart cried, and filled a poaching pan with water, which he quickly brought to a boil, then carefully lowered the egg into one of four rounds. Shortly, he stood before the customer with the dropped egg of perfect consistency, soon to bleed sun-like on the buttered toast. The stranger looked up and grinned.

"We miss you at The Bell," he simpered.

The customer lowered his head to eat.

"The persimmon trees in the park are lovely in wintertime, Mr. Hart. I'll draw our bath and await you under the El."

The restroom door opened, and the counterman, the News sticking out of his back pocket, resumed his station. Bird blew the last bar of "Ornithology." Hart, stricken, leaned against the grill and stared out into the night.

"Can I get you anything else?" the counterman asked.

"Not this time," the stranger replied. And rose to leave, humming to the chef:

"Bloody Whitey on our Sails, Spinoza. I'll hold the moo."

When Eli finished speaking, he began laughing to himself with unusual zest. *Where was all this headed?* The story of course wasn't Ishmael's or one that Eli had imagined; it was yet another one I'd written years earlier during a period in my life I preferred not to revisit.

Had I inadvertently become an accomplice in the young man's descent across the proverbial River Styx?

But why this tale? Is it an effort to interact with me on a more subliminal level? As he read aloud, the memory of being shadowed by that sadist provoked terror inside me, just as it had years earlier. Had Eli been scarred by such an incident in MacLeish Sq.? Or was it merely one storyteller applauding another?

From the beginning, when Eli indirectly referenced my brother's fate in his Fubar tale, it had become evident to me that each of his narrative recitations veiled his intent.

Above his desk he'd pinned a copy of Gustave Dore's illustration of the wrathful and sullen in Canto VII.

*Now we are sullen in this black ooze'—where
they hymn this in their throats with a gurgling sound*

because they cannot form the words down there.

To it Eli had appended this verse, underlining the lamentations that couldn't break through in words. An anguish that had no vocabulary.

It spoke to the young man's inability to explain what had befallen him. As if he had lost the lexicon that would permit him to seek a way out of the brackish waters of ill-reason to which he feared succumbing.

Perhaps he saw the *Inferno* as a guide, together with Virgil and Dante...

> *We entered on that hidden road to find*
> *Our way once more into the world of light.*
> *My leader walked ahead and I behind...*[i]

I ventured a guess as to why he was seeking a path into my past through my journals.

They were ballast, just as the texts of Dante and Melville had become for him. The tongue benumbed to the voice only its victim can hear.

I even happened upon him in the cellar one morning where I have a workbench and sundry woodworking tools.

He had taken a balsa wood box that had once held a bottle of wine and had shaped one end of it to resemble the bow of a boat. The box was joined on all three sides with its top secured by miniature brass hinges. With an electric engraving tool, Eli was burning onto the lid what appeared to be hieroglyphics.

No stranger now to the texts he was reading, I saw that it was a crude rendering of Queequeg's coffin in *Moby-Dick*, which at the novel's close had ferried Ishmael, the *Pequod's* lone survivor, to shore.

> *With a wild whimsiness, he now used his coffin for a sea-chest; and*
> *emptying into it his canvas bag of clothes, set them in order there.*
> *Many spare hours he spent, in carving the lid with all manner of gro-*

tesque figures and drawings; and it seemed that hereby he was striving, in his rude way, to copy parts of the twisted tattooing on his body. And that tattooing, had been the work of a departed prophet and seer of his island, who, by those hieroglyphic marks, had written out on his body a complete theory of the heavens and the earth, and a mystical treatise on the art of attaining truth; so that Queequeg in his own proper person was a riddle to unfold; a wondrous work in one volume; but whose mysteries not even himself could read, though his own live heart beat against them . . .[ii]

"I'm curious as to why Queequeg has captured your imagination, Eli."

"For the same reason he captured Ishmael's," was his clipped response.

"Why was that?"

Without looking up from his work, Eli muttered, "'He would gladly die for me, if need should be.'"

Stunned by the Ishmael quote, I took it as an indirect message to me, for each of us was acutely alive to the irony of how Ishmael's prophesy played out when Queequeg's coffin became the narrator's life-buoy.

Would I become Eli's?

It was a test. If I hadn't verbally acknowledged his reply, I knew he would take that as a noncommittal.

In turn I quoted from the same passage:

Through all his unearthly tattooings, I thought I saw the traces of a simple honest heart . . . content with his own companionship; always equal to himself . . . I'll try a pagan friend, thought I, since Christian kindness has proved but a hollow courtesy. iii

I asked Eli if I had passed.

He held up his model coffin with its modified bow. "Do you think *Pequod's* carpenter would've painted it?"

"Shellacked," I quipped.

Once the lights were doused in our bedroom that night, with notable haste he returned to his MacLeish Sq. narrative. It wasn't until several minutes passed that I began to decipher his reason.

"A couple weeks after I began to be tutored by the Stove-Boat Ishmael in *the book*, I happened to see him from a distance as I was walking down by the harbor alone. It was an hour or so after midnight. I had been unable to sleep. Often one could see an armada of ghost-like boats offshore. It was difficult to make out their hulls in the pitch black, but each was defined by a smattering of pale amber lamps that because of the wave action caused them to appear insect-like from afar.

"I moved out of Ishmael's line of sight. He walked to the edge of the wharf and after a few moments I saw what appeared to be one of those illuminated hulls begin to move toward shore. Then I eyed in a small skiff a man rowing with another seated in its stern. Shortly Ishmael was accompanying this passenger, shrouded in a white garment, up Hester Alley toward the Basilica.

"The very next morning, as a number of us gathered in the Sq., we happened upon Ishmael and the very same stranger engaged in deep conversation.

"My tutor motioned for me to come and sit alongside the pair.

"This is what I heard the stranger relate."

Eli reached down at the side of his bed and began reading from a notebook.

Mama gestured that I sit down. She walked over to the kitchen window and stared out over our back yard. "Your Uncle Paul always kept to himself. Grandmother bought him an old church piano when he was a boy, and that's how he entertained himself. Always at the keyboard, composing his own tunes. Because he was so unlike any of the rest of us, we called him brilliant.

"His friends were all inside his head. When we got our first television set, he'd watch *The Liberace Show*. When the program was over, he'd sit at the upright and began mocking the pianist. Except not for Mother's or my pleasure—for his imaginary companions. So, I simply ignored him."

"Did he care?"

"No. On his twenty-first birthday Paul gathered up all his compositions that he'd penciled on staff paper and hesitated at the door like he didn't know whether to say goodbye."

"'Where you headed to, Paul?' Grandma asked. He kept eying her until she lowered her head and said, 'Stay out of the rain, Son. Button up when it gets cold. If you change your mind . . .' By then he'd wandered off."

"You ever see him again, Mama?"

"Once. There were carolers on town square one Christmas Eve. It was snowing heavily, and several of us on last-minute errands gathered round to listen. That statue of General Grant? Well, I looked over and spotted Paul, dressed all in white, sitting at the general's feet.

"'Paul, it's me, Margaret,' expecting him to ignore me or walk away. Instead, he stood up.

"'Maggie, how good to see you! Have you found a man yet?'

"I stared at him, dumbfounded.

"'Merry Christmas,' he continued. 'If I would've known . . .' Like he felt he had to give me a gift. Suddenly, the tears that I never shed for him began to well up inside me.

"'Oh, please don't cry, Maggie. I live in a wonderful place in the woods. A little room I've built with tree limbs, straw, canvas awnings, tin signs, and abandoned doors, and . . . well, nearly anything I could find. I keep out of the rain mostly and sleep well. When the snow begins to fly, I move into my winter house, one near the brick-yards. The kilns always burn there, so it's quite pleasant.'

"'Do you have friends, Paul?'

"'Oh no.' I could see he was becoming anxious.

"'They're not like you and me, Maggie. You can't trust any of 'em.'

"'Paul, could we meet again? I'll buy you a chili dog at Coney Island. You know, like when we were kids?'

"I reached out to touch his hands. But he pulled them stiffly to his sides and turned away.

"'Tell Mama, Maggie.'

"'What?'

"'Not to get rid of my piano.'

"'But it's gathering dust in the living room,' I said.

"'No. I play it every night. *Haven't you heard?*'"

Periodically, Eli would glance up to see if I was alert to his purpose. Like before, it was as if we were corresponding in code—one of his own choosing, but with my words—for once again he'd lifted a section from one of my stories.

I perceived that if he were to ask me straight out what was on his mind, he trusted that he would never get the full story. That it had to be cosseted in the ambiguity of fiction. For Eli, reality was a fabricator. His years in MacLeish Sq. confirmed that for him.

The layers of separation between the young man and myself were incalculable. Except they weren't.

"Was there an Uncle Paul in *our* family?" he asked.

"Had my story convinced you that he was real?" I replied.

"It's why I ask."

"Then he was. Alive as the voice at the foot of your bed."

Eli nodded as if he understood.

"The white garments," he said, "it's how my father will be dressed when we meet, isn't it?"

I couldn't respond.

Lifting his dog-eared copy of *Moby-Dick* from his bedside, he read:

> *And from the pallor of the dead, we borrow the expressive hue of the shroud in which we wrap them. Not even in our superstitions do we fail to throw the same snowy mantle round our phantoms; all ghosts rising in a milk-white fog—Yea, while these terrors seize us, let us add that even the kind of terrors, when personified by the evangelist, rides on his pallid horse. (Revelation 6.8: "And I looked, and behold a pale horse: and his name that sat on him was Death, and Hell followed with him.)* [iv]

I struggled to not be overcome by Eli's darkness and couldn't help but recall Ishmael describing Starbuck, *Pequod's* first mate, ignite a lamp and hand it to his squire, Queequeg, as a "standard bearer of this forlorn hope" while they pursued harpooning the White Whale.

> *There then he, Queequeg, sat holding the imbecile candle in the heart of that mighty forlornness. There then he sat, the sign and symbol of a man without faith, holding up hope in the midst of despair.* [v]

In this very moment, I, John Proctor, saw myself as Queequeg . . . for like Ishmael, I had come to view the universe as a "vast practical joke." Yet how could I not hold the lit "imbecile" candle before the young man?

Was Eli, in the end, destined to be my life-buoy?

I gestured that Eli continue the Uncle Paul reading. "Except pretend that it is *your* story now, son. Convince me that he is your relative and not mine."

He eyed me, befuddled, then unselfconsciously embraced the challenge.

Whereupon I watched him transpose what had fired my imagination decades earlier. Eli became my narrator whose uncle had become a source of inspiration.

Queequeg's light flickered iridescent. We could even see Charon's amber eyes. They frightened neither of us in our bedroom that night.

* * *

Dominick and I were in the seventh grade, except he should have been in the tenth. "They lock you in until you are sixteen—or until you run off loony into the woods," he said.

"That's what I want to talk to you about," I said.

We thought visiting my Uncle Paul would be kind of neat, figuring that folks like him didn't separate from the townsfolk because of us kids. It was the grown-ups they couldn't abide.

"Can you imagine, Dom, how terrific it'd be to sleep by the open brick kilns when snow's flying? All those open fire pits. And, in springtime, living in a little camp house we've made from screen doors and old root beer signs, havin' our own bed and pet squirrels and birds and any comic books we ever wanted right out in the open. Never having to worrying about somebody saying no. How bad could it be? Wasting our lives like here in this damn old brick school building every day?"

Eli read as if he were nostalgically reflecting on his own childhood.

Dominick pulled out a pack of smokes. "You want one, Ethan?"

He inhaled like a grown-up. Why I liked him so much. Had the guts to do things I didn't. Like playing hooky. Or going out to the fringes of town and seeing how the crazies really lived. Maybe even discovering that they were smarter than the rest of us.

"'Cause my Uncle Paul's no dummy, Dominick. Mama said he was a virtuoso piano player who had an encyclopedio mind."

"What's that?"

"Like he got a bookcase of dictionaries stuck in his head."

"You mean like a walkin' library?"

"Somethin' like that."

"Jesus. I just got pictures of naked women up in my noggin.

"Ethan, whaddaya say you and me, tomorrow morning, take our school lunches and head out lookin' for your Uncle Paul. You say he plays the piano? Christ, wouldn't that be somethin' to go into the woods 'n' hear Liberace?"

Then Dominick turned serious.

"Your uncle ain't no queer, is he, Ethan?"

"Shit, I ain't ever thought about that," I said.

"What the hell," he sniffed. "If he's too friendly with us, we'll back off. Ain't scared of women. Why should I fear queers?"

I nodded in agreement.

"Where do you think Uncle Paul's place is, Ethan?"

I liked that Dominick was now calling him Uncle Paul. "Ain't sure, but if I was gonna move to the outskirts of town like him, I'd live near Cascade Park. So, in the summertime I could watch the roller coaster loop through the gorge and be near Candle Lake, where after dark I could swim and maybe even borrow a skiff at the rental dock. I sure understand someone wantin' to get off by themselves . . . but not too far."

We made plans to head off after the first tardy bell in the morning.

* * *

Cascade Park was a couple miles out in the country. "We're gettin' closer," Dominick said. "Keep your eye out for old shacks, abandoned cars, stuff like that."

It was early springtime, a couple months before the amusement park would officially open. The dodgem cars were in storage, and the carousel horses had been removed for fresh painting. The ice hadn't completely thawed on Candle Lake.

We passed the Lake Erie and Lackawanna railroad tracks and spotted an abandoned caboose sitting off on a sideline.

Dominick's eyes lit up. "That's somebody's home!" he cried. A weathered blouse was curtaining its window. Dominick ran ahead. Within several yards of the caboose, he held a finger to his lips, waving for me to hurry up. "Somebody's in there," he whispered, gesturing that I lean over so he could step on my back to peer into the window.

When he stepped back onto the ground, I asked what he'd seen.

"Those pictures I told you of naked broads inside my head?"

"Yeah."

"Take a peek." He bent over so I could climb onto his back.

I couldn't see a damn thing inside that caboose except for cardboard boxes and grocery sacks stuffed with old clothes.

"You're full of shit," I said.

"But it sure as hell beats goin' to class and worryin' decimal points, huh?"

Eli looked up. "Dominick isn't real, is he?"

"As real as you are pretending to be him," I replied.

He nodded and resumed reading.

When we arrived at the park, Dominick wanted to make believe we were riding the dodgems. We ran around inside the open-air building, honking and bumping into each other until we lay exhausted on its metal floor, laughing.

At the carousel he made organ noises and had me climb on his shoulders like he was my brightly painted steed and trotted around the circular platform, rising up and down, until he collapsed with me—dizzy as hell. He pulled out another Lucky Strike, lit it, took a drag, then passed it to me.

My first smoke. Jesus, it was heaven.

When he insisted we climb the scaffolding of the roller coaster that dipped treacherously into the gorge, I begged off and watched him mount the Cannon Ball's track to begin climbing. He waved his bandanna, hollering to me from its highest peak.

Then he disappeared, running down the other side like he was its first car.

In the prior year, two grade-school boys had leaped to their deaths out of one of its cars where a nest of rattlesnakes had taken up residence.

I believed somebody like my friend would never die.

Eli paused once again. *Had he known a Dominick in his past?*

I took a seat inside the unlocked carousel ticket booth and waited when I saw him coming up the midway in a kiddie fire truck. It had no wheels and he was inside, walking it forward.

"Look what I found!"

Its paint was scaling, and the body was also missing its puny ladders, but the silver bell on its hood still had its clapper, and Dominick had tied his belt to the bell, yanking it.

"Ethan, we'll take it home, put wheels on it, and hook it up to a gasoline Maytag washin' machine's motor. Jesus, ain't it a beaut?"

"Did you steal it from one of the kiddie rides?"

"Hell no. It was in a junk heap."

"Time to eat," I said.

Dominick stretched out alongside his fire engine and ate a bean sandwich. Mine was bologna with mustard, and I shared my orange.

"We'd just be headin' to music class," he muttered.

"Then arithmetic." I shuddered.

"Then, praise Jesus, the goin'-home bell. The happiest sound in all the world, right, Ethan?"

I looked around at the empty midway and wintered rides. "Do you think any of the fringe people wander through here off season? Like a graveyard, if you ask me."

Dominick nodded. "Do you suppose Uncle Paul wanders through here? You think he might play the carousel music in his head and imagine the painted horses galloping up and down with kiddies on 'em?

"And the Ferris wheel over there. Does he picture himself in the seat at the very top, swinging back and forth while lookin' back over our town and all the folks he's left behind . . . like your mama, for instance?"

Dominick had pulled out another cigarette and offered me one. We both lit up.

"You think he has a friend like you or me, Ethan?"

"Mama said he only talked to himself."

"Shit. No dodgem buddy to honk out of the way or bang into, huh? And who'd climb on my back when I wanted to play merry-go-round? Or share a peek of the naked lady inside the red caboose?"

He stood up.

"Let's go back, Ethan, before the goin'-home bell rings."

"Don't you want to check out the woods, Dom, to see if we can spot Uncle Paul?"

"Not today."

He walked on ahead of me toward town.

"What are you gonna tell your mama when the school principal lets her know, Ethan?"

"The truth."

"Mine won't give a shit," he said.

We walked on until the houses began to reappear.

Dominick turned to me.

"It beats school, though, right, Ethan?"

"Hell yes."

"You know how to smoke now, and maybe the next time your head will be chock full of pretty pictures like mine."

"Better than an old encyclopedio mind," I shot back.

Eli folded the sheaf of papers and placed them at the side of his bed.

"You going to finish?" I asked.

"I'd prefer not to."

"Why?"

"I read the story. Why kill him off?"

He turned off his headboard light. Our room now lay in total darkness. No headlights circling the walls of our bedroom or the ceiling. Each of us knew the other was wide awake.

"Why kill him off?"

When I was a boy, I read to my kid brother, Jeremiah. At each day's end we were sent to bed accompanied by a stern command for "lights out." Once he believed Momma thought we were settled in for the night, he'd bring out a flashlight then reach under the bed for one of his story books. He had a couple of favorites that I read over and over, sometimes on successive nights. And I'd say, "But where's the mystery, Jeremiah? Jesus, we know how it's going to end. Why, you could recite the whole book without our ever turning the flashlight on."

Except his friends were all getting under the covers with him. There'd be no surprises, for they never died like he feared he might before daybreak.

But then came the day Jeremiah was no longer interested. The illustrated books gathered dust under our bed, the flashlight batteries expired, and our estrangement had cast a pall over our room.

Now only the parish bells for evening Mass signaled the prelude to darkness.

Several minutes transpired before I heard Eli reach down to retrieve the story.

"Here, you finish it," he said.

"But I like hearing you, son."

"Who are we kidding?"

I switched on my bedside lamp and began reading:

After our outing it wasn't so much Dominick not wanting to hang around with me, but his feeling that he made me uncomfortable with his grown-up ideas . . . that he could see through my bravado.

When he'd pass me in the hallways, he'd ask, "You seen Uncle Paul?"

"Bumped into him on the dodgem," I'd jape.

One day he pulled me over after school, absolutely lit up with excitement.

"Ethan, I think I found him!"

"Yeah? Holy Jesus, where?"

"Nowhere close to the park. He's living out near the dam."

The notorious Cement Dam rose on the southern outskirts of

Hebron. Decades earlier the town fathers planned to reroute the Shenango River that ran through town and, instead, flood acres of lowland to create a manmade lake and stock it with trout and bass. They constructed this huge cement dam to hold the river back, but for reasons impossible to sort out, the project was never completed, and the Shenango continued to flow in the path it had from time immemorial.

Over the years, Cement Dam, because of its enormous height, became a favorite leaping-off place for those townsfolk determined to end their lives. Each year the Hebron Patriot would report on one or two citizens found dead at its base—most often in the fall and winter months.

Surrounded by woods amid a vast field, it rose like an abandoned movie set, a concrete barrier towering hundreds of feet into the air . . . and no river in sight.

So those who didn't opt to take up residence on the outskirts of town often found their way after dark to the top of the embankment and plunged.

"I found a small hut near the dam, Ethan," Dominick continued. "The size of one of our schoolrooms. Its roof is made of tin soda pop signs with its walls tethered together with house doors, pieces of tar paper, canvas and an entrance made of burlap sacks. It's got no windows.

"I thought—*That's Uncle Paul's house. Surer than hell.* I'm gonna take off school Monday. Maybe you want to join me?"

He picked up on my hesitation right off. "On second thought, you better let me check him out first. Bein' you probably look like your mama, it might upset him." He put his hand on my shoulder like we were still friends. "I'll report back to you, buddy."

I wanted to tell my mother. Except I didn't. And for several nights prior to Monday morning—the day Dominick was headed back out to Cement Dam—I fantasized about the two of them meeting.

Uncle Paul and my friend heading to the midway, and Dominick pretending that he was buying tickets for the Cannon Ball, the biggest and scariest roller coaster this side of Cleveland, Ohio. Maybe he'd hoisted Uncle Paul on his shoulders and play the carousel horse, the one that looked like a unicorn, whose hoofs were gentian violet. Or Uncle Paul would take Dominick for a ride in the orange dodgem and crash into, one by one, his imaginary friends. Or Dom might bring out the kiddie fire truck that we never dragged home and let Uncle Paul pretend to ride it back to his tin-and-tar-paper shack . . . and the two of them would sit inside when it began to rain and talk about why they left home . . . and school.

Where Uncle Paul had an encyclopedio mind . . . Dominick had a gasoline-combustion engine and *wemen* in his and was always on the go, looking for new excitement. I thought together they could make one very real human being.

Each night I'd imagine more and have the most peaceful sleep ever.

* * *

That coming Monday, like he said, Dominick didn't show up for class. I waited outside in the schoolyard after the final bell. When it began to get dark, I walked home.

Tuesday, I didn't pass him in the hallways.

Wednesday either.

On Thursday we all were summoned into the auditorium. Principal McCallister stepped out on the dais and cleared his throat. Several teachers were standing behind him, glancing down at their shoes. One was Mrs. Gresham, whose class Dominick and I both loved because he and I had been in her rhythm band (he played the castanets; I, the sand blocks). My friend was taller than Mrs. Gresham and could've been her husband. She was tearing up and dabbing her cheeks with a lace hanky.

"Boys and girls, I've very sad news to report. Your classmate Dominick Scorcini was found dead on the outskirts of our town last evening, the victim of foul play. He'd been reported missing since Monday."

McCallister took a deep breath, and several girls in the audience began crying.

I was too shocked. What did "foul play" mean? All I could picture was my friend running back and forth over the lip of the Cement

Dam, yelling into the hollow below, waiting for his echo to bounce back to him.

Was that foul play?

The evening paper printed a photograph on its front page of the tin sign and tar paper shack just as Dominick had described it. Staring fiercely into the Patriot photographer's lens and beyond, the fringe man had long, black hair and a beard resembling a bird's nest. He wore several layers of soiled rags that once had been real garments. Cloth and leather tethered with clothesline covered his feet.

Alongside stood the Hebron police captain, holding on to the man's arms like he'd been chasing him and finally caught up.

Dominick had been snooping around the hovel when inside a pair of eyes had a bead on him. When my friend had begun circling closer, threatening he was about to lift its burlap sack door, somebody's uncle pulled the shotgun's trigger.

But it wasn't Paul.

Visualizing Dominick lying there dead, I realized that I could have been lying alongside him. All the pictures of the naked women would be bleeding out of his head onto the yellow grass.

And school would resume tomorrow.

"Thank you," Eli muttered.

I switched off the light.

At some point in the night, I was awakened by a rustling noise. Eli had climbed out of bed and was putting his clothes on.

"Where are you going?"

"To hunt for Uncle Paul."

I rose and began dressing, hoping to keep him engaged.

"*Dominick bleeding images of naked women onto the dry grass . . .* that mawkish shit's for mortals, Eli. Don't you understand?"

Fevered with anxiety, he turned at the bedroom door and jeered: "You know what happened to *Pequod's* Black shipmate's source of 'jolly cleverness'?"

"Yes," I answered.

"Cast into the water once while an oarsman on the whale boat and quickly rescued. Second time overboard he drifted out of sight and only after a long period of time by the 'merest chance' rescued. Yet back on board the *Pequod . . .*"

Eli exclaimed: "Pip went about the deck an idiot, for Chrissake!

He saw God's foot upon the treadle of the loom and spoke it; and there-fore, his shipmates called him mad. So, man's insanity is Heaven's sense."[vi]

"In Ishmael's side chapel, were those lines drilled into you?"

It was as if I'd suddenly confused him, drawing him back to MacLeish Sq.

"I want you to take me there one day, son."

The young man's expression registered abject disbelief.

"Whenever you are prepared. Tomorrow or weeks from now."

He continued to stare at me, gauging my sincerity.

I gave him no berth.

Within moments he sat down on his unmade bed. "I must think about it."

"Thank you, Eli."

I returned to my bed and drew the covers up. It wasn't long after that I heard him climb back into his.

It had passed.

Yet outside our door that night I imagined Pip's "gloomy-jolly" beating the death march on his tambourine, accompanying his lamentations of lunacy, while Queequeg tried out his final resting place for comfort.

* * *

We awoke at daybreak and at breakfast neither of us broached our conversation hours earlier. I set about resuming work, and from my studio window observed Eli sitting in the sun on our back porch and reading.

Having become absorbed by his will to communicate indirectly as a means of getting closer to the essence of what he was seeking, I began to understand this manner of approaching "truth."

Take the Uncle Paul story, for instance. The piece conveyed the narrator's suspicion that the Uncle who separated himself from society carried within his consciousness a more revealing verity, whereas his mother and the townspeople were lesser off because of it.

Yet after briefly indulging in that narrative, Eli scornfully turned on it, labeling it a "kid's story."

He sought the deeper more universal truth in Melville's Pippin.

I couldn't take issue with my housemate's insight. I had scribbled a children's tale.

His sixth sense far exceeded mine, permitting me the quiet gratification of accompanying him to an uncertain resolution.

Yet, the paradox.

I was now enmeshed in our combined fates.

Having committed to follow Eli to MacLeish Sq. subjected me

to the possible resurrection of my own Mephisthophelean voice. For to confront his *Neverland*, to visit there and entertain its inhabitants, I was knowingly countenancing the young man's imminent madness. Still, I had to accompany Eli into the fire if I hoped to save him from being devoured by it.

CHAPTER FOUR

ELI

I relished crossing the Charles Bridge to meet with Ishmael in his other guise.

Had he other young acolytes like myself to whom he showed deference in the same discreet manner? I wondered.

Some weeks after I learned about his being a short order cook in a New York City eatery, he and I were sitting alongside each other at the Stove Boat's counter when he inquired about my past, spare as it was.

"Not much to offer," I said.

"Then make it up."

I laughed.

"What do you think I'm tutoring you in—*the Melville bible*? Thread the truth with a fabrication and begin weaving your past, boy. You want to become an Ishmael one day, I presume?"

I nodded.

"Well, then, let me hear."

And from my notebook, I read to him about my mother's friend.

His name was Horace, about forty years old, same as Mother, the only child of Mrs. McCool in the neighboring house. I hadn't seen Mother in some time. When I stopped by to visit—she'd moved again—we sat outside on the porch. "I should call Horace to come down and see you," she said.

Mother called him like she was calling a dog out of the woods.

"Horace!" she yelled. "Come on down here. I want you to meet young Eli."

Soon I heard a screen door slam.

"You hear?" she said. "Talk to him like you might anybody. Uncle Ed, say."

Well, I'd met the man a couple years earlier and knew he wasn't my real uncle. He drove an ice cream truck and he'd give me a Klondike bar and regale me with off-color stories. Claimed he came by Mother's house every day for lunch and would sit with her on the mohair sofa in our living room. After, he'd eat an egg sandwich and have his coffee. Sometimes after dark, too, he said. Then begin laughing.

Ed was portly and he wasn't too bright like she said Horace was. "Horace can recite history better than any book you read in school, Eli."

Mother had started to flutter. First it was her hands. Now I noticed it had crept up her arms.

Well, when I saw Horace, he looked normal enough, excepting he was skinny, had long hair, and his arms moved independent of his mind. He loped down through the beech trees. Under one arm were several composition books, and in the pocket of his shirt, ink pens and pencils were lined up. He wore gold-rimmed glasses with thick, clouded lenses.

"This is Eli, Horace. He's a bright young boy. Like you, Horace. He's also very special to me, just like you. I told him you know more history than his schoolbook. That in truth you know more dates and numbers and facts than any single book in the whole wide world! Ain't that right?"

Horace blushed and turned away, sounding an embarrassed chortle. He lifted his feet up and down on the grass rhythmically. It was then I spotted his right ear—it'd grown back into Horace's head like a bellybutton.

"Ask Horace a question, Eli."

We'd been studying the Civil War in grade school. "General Sumpter," I said.

"General Sumpter?"

"Yes."

"His wife or his children? Their ages or their names? His house or its acreage? His battles, their dates, casualties—men or horses—or their rations?"

Mother interrupted. Crimson was rising into his face fast as if he were about to explode in frustration. She told me later she was afraid he'd scream and begin running through their woods.

"Eli, don't confuse Horace! The questions must be very precise.

"How tall was General Sumpter, Horace?" she volunteered. "That's what the boy wants to know."

"Six feet four inches," came the rapid response with a grand sigh. Like the air coming out of one of Uncle Ed's tires on his sporty Ford coupe with the spoke wheel attached to its trunk.

"Was he handsome, Horace?"

"Very handsome, ma'am. Blue eyes and soldierly bearing. Size twelve shoes and walked with a slight limp. Not a war injury. A farm implement injury—a harrow. His wife's name was Emma. They had twelve children, Sadie, Beatrice . . ."

At that point Mother again interrupted. "That's fine, Horace. You did very well." Horace blushed again, going into his little tap routine on the grass, turning the knotted ear to both of us like a cyclopean eye. I sat down in the grass, Horace alongside me. He moved close.

"Are you my friend?" he asked.

"Yes," I answered after glancing up to Mother to see how I should respond.

"Fine," he said. "I like scholars."

Mother nodded.

Then told me she'd be down in the kitchen if I needed anything, leaving me there in the tall grass with Horace.

"Two scholars," he kept repeating matter-of-factly like he was cementing sod in the earth, tamping it down to get a firm hold. Then he held out two pencils, a red one and blue one, asking me to take the one I wanted. He handed me a composition book. I opened it up and there were letters and numbers in very orderly columns but at random angles across each of its pages. The letter Q followed by a 3865, say, then a grouping of letters—some upper case, some lower, with no definable pattern emerging, trailed by the numbers again. Nothing in any order apparent to me. No series of letters spelled a word—backward, forward or jumbled—that I knew. But they were written with a most careful hand, like a scrivener's, page after page.

As I leafed through the book, he watched me intently. I was careful to show no emotion. Finally, I looked up to see if I could fathom some reason in his eyes for these hundreds and hundreds of columns, almost as if they were thin glass vials in which he had dropped a number, a series of letters, then more numbers, a letter and a number and so on to the vial's rim, then capped the cylinder to begin a new one. Test tube cylinders, perhaps. Page after page, all in pencil.

Horace beamed when I looked at him. Immensely proud of what he had achieved.

"This is magnificent, Horace."

We were sitting but his feet began to twitch as if they were shuffling that embarrassed dance again, and the belly-knot ear swung round to eye me like a searchlight.

"Eli," he said. "Only Horace can do this. Nobody in this whole wide world . . ." and he gestured back to his house and then to Mother's, then off to the woods and the dirt street. "Only Horace McCool can do this. Come," he said, "I'll teach you. And he flipped open to one of the blank pages in my composition book. "I've saved that one for you."

He opened his book to a fresh page.

"Just begin," he said. "First . . ." he looked up into Mother's willow tree, "a . . . G!" he cried.

I wrote a G.

"329810!" These came in a rush.

I columned these. He cast a critical eye over my work. I had written 32 under the G. This upset him. He erased it, wrote the three, then the two under the three.

"Okay," he said.

And that's how we spent that afternoon in the grass. Writing random numbers and letters into his "journals." Toward the end of our sessions, he looked exhausted.

"Are you tired?" I asked.

I could see the sun beginning to fall behind Mother's house. The
sweat had gathered on both our bodies, and the flies were becoming
pesky. Horace slapped at them, anguished, as if they were meddle-
some children who wouldn't leave us alone.

"Yes," he said, "very tired."

"Let's put the journals away for today, Horace."

"Yes, let's," he said. I gathered his pencil and mine, placed them
back in his shirt pocket exactly in the order they came. I stood up,
then reached down to lift him out of the tall grass.

He turned to walk slowly back toward Mother McCool's house.
Like he was dead tired.

"I'll tell my class I met General Sumpter's historian in the woods
today, Horace!" I hollered up to him. He turned his head so that
I saw the deformed ear. Down in the grass where we had been sitting that long afternoon, it looked like a deer or a lion or perhaps a
bear had napped. The day was ending. Shortly Uncle Ed would stop
by. She and he would disappear into the darkened living room. The
shades were always drawn when I walked through her house.

I could hear Uncle Ed laughing, sweet-talking Mother; her rejoinder would always be a gentle, "Please."

I'd think about Klondike bars and General Sumpter and Horace with the belly-button ear and the spot in the field where the
tall grass had been tamped down and where Horace and I sat . . .
thinking somebody had lain there in the hot afternoon and the sun
rolled down over Mother's hill and her hurrying Ed on and him
chortling, riding her down into the old wire-spring sofa lunchtime,
dinnertime, and Horace, up in his shuttered house with Mother
McCool, building glass cylinders of random numbers and letters in
column containers, some code he alone understood, one ear already
turned inward.

I'd go back inside Mother's house upon hearing her in the kitchen.

"Your Uncle Ed's taking a nap on the sofa. We must be quiet. How
did you like Horace?" she asked.

I looked out her window beyond an aged willow tree, seeing the
day die, and became afraid of the oncoming night. Watching Horace tiredly lope back through the trees toward home to the darkened

Mother McCool's house, it bubbling inside me sad... Christ, it all felt so hollow, like I was spinning away from earth ... and I'd hear Uncle Ed snoring on the mohair sofa and watch her bent over the stove in the darkening kitchen, fry pan of eggs all twirled together, her shuddering, her feet almost dancing like Horace's when he blushed.

I wanted it to stop.

"It must be time for you to go back, Eli," she said. *Uh huh*, I thought.

"Okay," I answered. "Thanks for the wonderful day."

She'd nodded just like Horace. Still stirring the eggs in the black skillet. Never looking up. Her dance on the linoleum floor more agitated.

I walked through the shadowy streets of Naumkeag on my way home. And that night I dreamed about the battle of General Sumpter but saw Horace, with his knotted ear, in Calvary attire. Behind him were all these medics carrying litters. Horses dragging litters. On these litters were columns of numbers and letters. But the columns were bent and twisted. They were broken. Single numbers and letters were falling, dripping on the battlefield's grass like blood. And General Horace's stony face, wounded, resigned, headed to the McCool house through the woods. In the background I could hear a dirge, a loud moaning sound, a mournful cry as if it rose out of the ground, and I looked up and saw General Horace McCool stop the procession, draw his left hand to cover his good ear, capping it.

Two nights later, I spied Mother alone on the street, all dressed up fancy as if she were headed to a dance. And I stood secreted in a doorway watching her. Like she was waiting for somebody. Except I knew she wasn't. At one point I swear she saw me and mouthed:

"Your mother's dead, Eli."

I sat down on the stone steps and cried unashamedly, trying to envision happy things. I saw Uncle Ed passing out Klondike bars at the wake. To Horace and me and all of Mother's friends. I saw a huge sunflower lifted from the back of her property lying next to her in the bier, casting its mustardy twilight on her cheeks. Her head no longing randomly shaking. And vials of colored water, violet, raspberry-red, and a sea-green, with ginger-brown stoppers, lying alongside her right hand. *A kind of watery resurrection, the water of the streams in heaven,* I thought . . . and the children eating ice cream bars, smiling, and saying goodbye to her and how we'd meet her up in the fields, up there next to Mrs. McCool's house, waiting for her to call the Horaces of this world to come out and play with us and take all our tears away.

To teach us the history of life. And just how goddamn blue General Sumpter's eyes really were.

Goodbye, dear Mother, I said. You knew his belly-button ear would never startle me. How I'd think it looked like a strange exotic flower, really. You knew how I'd never embarrass you or him. The Horace you wouldn't dare introduce to anyone else in our family.

And you also knew how quickly afternoons come to an end. That the Uncles of this world would soon arrive home. That you'd have to undress. Not in the grass, but on an umber-wool sofa you had bought on time twenty years earlier. Then, after, you'd stir up his eggs in the black skillet at dark.

Ishmael had his head lowered the entire time as I spoke.

"Why tell me this particular story, Eli?"

"Maybe I'm beginning to miss her . . . now that she's gone."

"Except she isn't, is she?"

I stood and walked to the diner's door—then turned, facing him. "No," I muttered.

Ishmael knew—how, I'm not sure.

It had to become apparent to the regulars of the Falling Man because her solitary presence on a Friday evening was not infrequent.

"You haven't spoken to her for some time, have you, Eli?"

"Our unexpressed covenant."

I spoke to him as if he were attired in his black robe, the ivory Queequeg coffin amulet glinting about his neck.

"I prefer to think of her as dead. Her inebriated heart understands why . . . and has the grace to respect it. Your namesake, up to the very end . . . did he not see his likeness in Ahab?"

Ishmael didn't respond.

We moved to a table. "Eli, I once watched the two of you in the

Falling Man when I took a bar seat alongside, being that it was the only one unoccupied. Yet it was as if you were total strangers."

"She never wished to shame me. Any number of men in MacLeish Sq. have known her. I begrudgingly admire her for not recognizing them either."

"Might it cross your mind that someone else in the square enjoys a covenant with her like the one you and she share?"

"Are we in the Basilica confessional, sir?" His imputation stung.

But my tutor didn't break eye contact.

"A missing father you suggest, perhaps?" I japed.

Ishmael nodded.

"Of course. Each time I enter the Falling Man, I think: *And where might he be sitting tonight?* Am I naive to think her occasional presence is for my sake when it could very well for that stranger toward whom she harbors lingering feelings?"

* * *

From afar that very evening I witnessed her exiting the tavern alone and couldn't help but wonder if she, like the other residents of the square, had gotten off one of the armada boats in the harbor to seek an identity.

Had she arrived in this place where the Puritan ghosts zealously worshiped religion and law equally to seek redemption, a repurchasing of her soul? Was her very presence in MacLeish Sq. a testament to the imaginative power of the encased-in-bronze author who aroused in our consciousness the fiery "rag of scarlet cloth" under her black garments?

Yet she had known numerous Dimmesdales. Could that be the reason why even the more upstanding men in the square, even an occasional Ishmael, shadow her as if both attracted and repelled? Always solitary, she kept company in public with no one. Those rendezvous were never acknowledged by either party.

I began to intuit that MacLeish Sq., settled by a *"grave, bearded, sable-cloaked, and steeple-crowned progenitor"[4]* who arrived with his *"bible and sword,"* was destined to give birth to a Hester Prynne. How fitting that upon arriving here, the Puritans first allotted parcels of land for the cemetery and the prison.

Was it any mystery that the only source of earthly light for the ascetic males had to be the wick of a woman's body?

In all my *Moby-Dick* tutoring sessions by Ishmael, there was scarce mention of the opposite sex. Yet but another reason why she, the Hester acolyte, owned a seductive presence in and around MacLeish Sq.

Consider the narrator's rare observation:

> . . . in Salem where they tell me young girls breathe such musk, their sailor sweethearts smell them miles offshore, as though they were drawing nigh the odorous Moluccas instead of the Puritanic sands.[vii]

In Naumkeag, the musk was embroidered red, and she, its alley's namesake, came out mostly at dark, the winds off the harbor shadowing her and her male acolytes. Her singular aura more pronounced, dominant, than numerous, black-robed Ishmaels.

The latter carried no light under their stygian cloaks.

Not a few of them and their disciples, however, felt most alive as she passed by, igniting their groins. And, like crows, lust scurried in the square's trees. While Minos, the connoisseur of sin, stood watch from the peak of *La Porte d'Enfer.*

I wondered, was my tutor looking on the night I watched her enter the Cotton Mather alone? Given how unlikely it was that she would have ever crossed its threshold.

As was customary, she wore a raven cloak, but her hair, normally gathered in a severe bun, now fell freely on its collar. And her shoes, coal-black leather, glistened as if freshly polished with lamp oil. She entered the "dowdy establishment whose waiting room

4 "I began to intuit that MacLeish Sq., settled by a 'grave, bearded, sable-cloaked, and steeple-crowned progenitor' who arrived with his 'bible and sword' . . ." *The Scarlet Letter*, Hawthorne's introduction, pp 126.

evidenced a yearning for a funereal past replete with potted palms, chintz overstuffed sofas and chairs missing their antimacassars" to vanish down the corridor leading to the banquet hall.

The one bordered off by a wall of French doors curtained in cerecloth . . . the *Souls of the Dead Dining Room.*

So as not to be seen, I entered the hotel from the service entrance and stood just off the corridor leading to its main kitchen, watching her remove her cloak and take a seat at one of the twelve fully dressed tables illuminated by candle lanterns. No one was in the room, not even Charon at the grand Bosendorfer.

What stunned me was that she was now the woman I had known decades earlier. Not that she had lost all those years, but time had appeared to grant her a reprieve, for she was exceedingly lovely and adorned in red chiffon with a pair of turquoise-inlaid combs embellishing her raven hair.

Motionless, she sat with her hands folded before her on the lace tablecloth—her lipstick muted as was the shade of her dress by the wan light.

For a moment I felt enmeshed in a reverie. What was I witnessing?

Would I be summoned to stand before her in Charon's dressing room?

Was she alive?

Caught in anxiety's grip, I witnessed several men in black sable-cloth hats and heavy overcoats entering the room and, upon dispatching their outer gear, accompanying her to the table.

Not a single soul exchanged glances with her or each other. She acted as if the encounter had happened before, exhibiting no sign of fear or concern. Her face mirrored that of the young woman who in my boyhood had nurtured and cared for me. And when I was by fear possessed—as I often was—I could find comfort in her composure.

Momentarily Charon appeared and took his place at the piano.

The grim gentleman at the head of the table, the one I recalled as Cotton Mather, stood and faced Charon.

"Please, Maestro, a melody for this wondrous occasion."

Disconcerting and dreamlike, he began playing the song I'd heard as a boy coming from her room once she had placed me in bed for the night: "My Haunted Heart"—a recording she played over and over most evenings.

I watched her expression catch the light as to why she had arrived at this occasion. It was Cotton Mather who reached over and took her hand and—in a wooden manner—proceeded to lead her about on the *Souls of the Dead Dining Room* parquet dance floor.

Like those nights long ago when she and I were alone in the house, it was as if the recording's female vocalist was walking ghost-like down the hallway outside my bedroom, up and down the stairs, yearning in a manner to which I was becoming accustomed. As if something elementary was missing in my mother. Over time, I sensed it was also lacking in me.

When Reverend Mather had finished, each of the other ashen gentlemen took their turns. Not one broke a smile, touched any part of her body except to grasp her hand, or betrayed the suggestion that he wafted the scent of musk rising from her person . . . or theirs.

Even Charon dared not cast a wistful glance in her direction.

Once the music ended and her last partner had taken his place at the table, she gathered her mantle. Charon helped her into it as the men stared straight ahead.

It was befitting of the assembled, a comely *Danse Macabre.*

She took leave without acknowledging there had been anyone else in the room.

I marveled at what I had just witnessed, for at no point did I detect any sign of her tremors. Nothing should mar the hallowed occasion, be it a place setting with a missing dessert fork, a goblet bearing a fingerprint, or the fair woman—center of august assemblage—whose right hand unwittingly kept time to a tune not of her choosing.

But once back on Hester Alley, she visibly quavered and gathered her cloak about her body while vanishing into the shadows of the harbor.

Had I been the only one in MacLeish Sq. to behold the event?

Evidently it had occurred at least once earlier, for those attending knew what was to transpire next. Not even Ishmael had alerted me as to what I might see.

Still, I suspect he knew.

For days I pondered what the occasion might signify.

Then I saw her once again, the very same person she had always been in the evenings I'd encountered at the Falling Man. Secure within herself, nursing a drink, and speaking with no one on either side of her. A nightly presence in black wool and a tight hair bun. Except that her right hand she now cradled in her lap and out of sight. Only when she raised her glass did the amber liquid tremble.

* * *

Seeing Ishmael's habit hanging in Basilica's side chapel—his Que-equeg amulet reflecting the prismatic stained-glass window light—I caught up with him across the Charles Bridge. As if the man's priestly role had become a shade burdensome, it was much easier to converse there. In the Stove Boat he was relaxed and laughed often.

Since he had been absent from MacLeish Sq. for several days, he inquired if anything of interest had occurred at the Falling Man. I said the tavern had been unusually quiet the nights I was in attendance, while citing some of the regulars . . . including her.

"All in black?"

I nodded. "At her customary place."

Sitting at the counter, we continued to engage in small talk, but I soon sensed that Ishmael was stalling, reluctant to broach an issue with me. He rose and poured each of us a cup of coffee yet kept mindlessly fiddling with the creamer as if debating with himself, but then he went for it:

"Eli, *The Scarlet Letter*?"

My disbelief of his naming Hawthorne's book struck me as comical given that he and his Ishmael brethren often cast a jaundiced eye when the book was mentioned by an unsuspecting MacLeish Sq. local, suggesting that they treated it as "popular fiction" and unworthy of serious consideration. "*So, that is what's under your robe,*" I mused. *Father Ishmael, esteemed tutor and scholar of Ahab and the White Whale, invoking Hester Prynne?*"

"You've read it, I'm sure."

"Several times, I confess." It was an effort to resist grinning.

"Yes, living here, how could you not have? Her nightly presence at the tavern . . ." his voice trailed off.

I'd no idea what he was implying.

"Eli, suppose she ceased wandering about the square. What then?"

Except he addressed the elongated mirror above the Stove Boat's counter.

Ishmael swung about on the stool to face me and blurted out:

"*Would Hester Prynne have danced with those men, I ask you?*"

So, he *had* watched her. His accusatory rage and distress striking.

It was at this moment I began to see through a glass darkly: Ishmael, not by chance, had chosen to instruct me in the Melville-*Moby-Dick* catechism. I was his star student in committing to memory MacLeish Sq.'s chosen text. Only now I visualized his robe and Queequeg amulet in the side chapel shorn of life, trappings from the Basilica's musty ecclesiastical trunk.

Prisoner to his person within, Ishmael proceeded to thunder:

"*What are Cotton Mather and his retinue without her?*"

"*What is the Falling Man if she fails to appear?*"

Then he stopped, gathered himself, and went behind the counter. Neither of us spoke for several minutes while Ishmael impulsively scoured the grill. Finally, and without exchanging eye contact . . .

"You must be hungry, Eli."

"I'm really not."

Once again Ishmael took a seat alongside. Chagrined, he placed his arm around me.

"Despite our silly robes and symbols, son, we abide in the woman's shadow.

"*She was who she wished to be that night and who they desired to touch, however virginally, as they circled the* Souls of the Dead Dining Room. *But lust beat life into their atrophied hearts. How they wished to ravish her in those secret chambers. And she goddamned well knew it. And that, my dear son, is why she danced with them. That, dear friend, is why our male hearts beat on her time.*

"Remove her and we revert to birdsong."

* * *

Was Ishmael my father?

As I left the Stove Boat and wandered back across Charles Bridge, I kept telling myself what a deluded notion it was. Yet I was not privy to what might have occurred between the pair prior to my residing in MacLeish Sq. And why had Ishmael spoken so cordially about my mother?

Chillingworth, who unexpectedly reappears in Hester Prynne's life, confesses:

"What had I to do with youth and beauty like thine own ... delude myself that intellectual gifts might veil physical deformity in a young girl's fantasy?"

"I felt no love nor feigned any," she replies, having been sentenced to wear the mark of shame for life. [viii]

Hester's words helped me better understand the woman I had known growing up.

I felt no love nor feigned any.

I viewed her resolve to indifference as means of remaining untouched.

To salvage the exposure of the person secreted inside her.

It's what, I believe, permitted her to grace MacLeish Sq. with the serene bearing she did. Or to sit in the same seat at the Falling Man, radiating a self-acquittal that was the envy of others.

> *"The scarlet letter had been her passport into regions where other women dared not tread. Shame, despair, solitude! These had been her teachers— stern and wild ones—and they made her strong, but taught her much amiss."*[ix]

CHAPTER FIVE

JOHN PROCTOR

The young man, it seemed, was fabricating his life from swatches of the books he read, his bittersweet memories, and an insuperable will to escape an inherited eager fatalism. I thought of Faulkner's *Light in August:* "But it's the dead folks who do him the damage."

A weight he was determined to escape by imagining his forbears other than who they were ... and thereby shedding the truth.

And, in the process, giving birth to himself?

This is what struck at my heart.

Eli was conceiving himself out of this skein of words and images. "We think not in words but in the shadows of words," Nabokov wrote.

"Could Ishmael be my father?" he asks.

"*Yes,*" I said to myself upon closing his journal. "*And so could I.*"

For at that very moment, I visualized Eli standing before me on that snow-covered morning we first met, uttering a son's incendiary rebuke:

"*Mother knows you.*"

The journal had been left in my studio on purpose. He had begun peeling back the layers.

I'd convinced myself that what I'd perceived as a scornful damning had perished for the young man. That I was no longer viewed as his "birth father who had once profaned his mother ... my daughter."

But now I understood that from the moment I welcomed him into my life I would be unable to escape, even from myself.

The middle of that very night I was awakened by piano music coming from below. Sitting up in bed, I saw that Eli's bed was empty. I walked out into the hallway. No lights had been turned on downstairs, and I wondered if he was playing the phonograph. While standing there, I heard the last few bars of Cole Porter's "Love for Sale" succeeded by an up-tempo "You Do Something to Me" and anticipated catching sight of Eli sitting in the darkened living room, listening. But when I reached the bottom of the stairs, the music stopped.

Instead, in the pallid skylight filtering through the farmhouse windows, I saw him seated motionless at the Chickering upright, his back to me, adorned in my black glossy-lapeled Tuxedo wedding jacket and red socks. Nothing else.

"What is it, son?"

Visibly agitated, he turned, trance-like.

"Come back to bed," I cajoled.

Eli rose from the piano stool and with both arms grandly gestured to the adjoining room.

"*Please, Maestro, a melody for this wondrous occasion!*"

Then, chilling me in his pitiless gaze.

"*Mother knows you, John Proctor.*"

Once I had accompanied him back to our room, I knew that Eli had just telegraphed what was soon to be revealed. In the shadowy guise of Charon, he was auguring what lay before the two of us.

The next day passed without incident, but that night, after we had bid each other goodnight and climbed into our adjoining beds, Eli sat up and read the following:

Edgar Giles grieved over the loss of his father, his brother, and his dog—the last to expire, under the dining room table during the night. When it came time for the morning walk, Fred didn't stir. At the burial service in his back yard that afternoon, Edgar keened so loudly that his neighbor peered over the stockade fence.

"Fred's dead," he sobbed.

"My condolences," the abutter said.

"I don't like how this show is closing."

"Could you explain?" asked the neighbor.

"We keep getting lighter." Edgar flapped his arms in the air to demonstrate. "Parts of us keep falling away. When we were children our fortunes grew. Babies came, along with sofas and automobiles, nieces, and nephews.

"Now it's the long goodbye." He glanced at Fred's grave. "He shadowed me during the day. He lay asleep in the sun puddles throughout my house. He answered the door. Barked when the phone rang. Ate the food I found disgusting—licked my face . . ."

Edgar sobbed some more.

He dropped to his knees, scooped a handful of soil from the newly covered grave, and brought it to his face.

"Father, brother . . . now Fred," he mumbled. "Once it was the sky."

That evening Edgar crawled under the table. *I'll sleep here only this evening*, he thought. *In remembrance of him.*

At some point during the night, he crawled out to Fred's water bowl. *How silly is this?* Yet, it was more comforting than lying upstairs in his double bed, mourning the dog's departure. *Perhaps this is the way we keep our loved ones alive. We embrace our memories of them. Assume their personas.*

He curled up close to the back door and heard rustling in the rear yard. A hedgehog, he guessed—and reflexively barked.

Oh, Christ . . . how absurd!

But it didn't seem all that bizarre. After all, hadn't he often played a woman to his estranged wife, Beatrice, when they made love?

"Loosen my tie, unbutton this stiff white shirt, Edgar, oh yes, unzip my fly," she'd whisper.

Neither of them thought their exchanging roles was depraved. Why, he'd even asked her to lick his nonexistent breasts.

Edgar wandered into the living room and stretched out in a puddle of moonlight.

How he missed Beatrice, too. No letters or phone calls. Her clothes, the summer dresses with the robust chrysanthemums she left hanging alongside his suits in the closet. Her open-toed shoes.

The pillbox hats with veils. Alongside his shaving cream, her cerulean vials of cologne and perfume sat in the medicine chest. He would sprinkle some on her side of the bed after dark . . . then dream she'd slipped into the boudoir to caress him.

A car stopped in front of the house. Edgar ran to the window, yapping. It felt perfectly normal.

At daybreak he was awakened by the newspaper landing on the front stoop. Just as Fred faithfully did each morning, Edgar butted the door open with his nose, clenched the paper in his teeth, carried it to the sunroom, dropped it at the base of his favorite chair—then stood, turned on the coffee pot, and read the day's news.

Later that morning he placed a slice of sod over Fred's grave and decided against memorializing it with a marker. "What's the sense?" he reasoned. *"Bone and flesh under that sod, the animal is alive within me. Why couldn't I have understood that sooner?*

"None of my loved ones have departed. They are alive inside of me. I simply must be more caring, calling on them more than I ever have. Why, even Beatrice, she will be inside there, too. Father, Brother Jed, Fred, and Beatrice. How fortunate am I? How blessed?"

Following lunch, he undressed, put on Beatrice's ankle-length saffron empire dress flowered with Japanese lanterns, slipped on a pair of her coral mules, spritzed cologne under his arms, and returned downstairs to prepare tea.

"Today we'll have my brother over. He and Beatrice always got along."

From the cupboard he chose a package of fancy tea cookies and placed several on a tole tray alongside the fragile porcelain teacups. In the living room he set them on the glass table with the ornate Oriental walnut base. A Matisse odalisque hung on the side wall. How charming, he thought, and settled into the plush sofa, awaiting Jed.

But Jed was late.

Soon he thought he heard steps on the front walk. He ran to the door and barked.

"My imagination," he said, and returned to the sofa.

Jed sat opposite him wearing Tasmanian worsted trousers, tassel loafers, and a Bengal-striped linen shirt with open collar.

"I've been expecting you, dear Jed," Edgar enthused. "It's been too long. I feared you'd never arrive."

Jed eyed Beatrice closely. Her narrow feet, their high instep, the scent of jasmine. Heady in the shadowy room.

"How lovely you look this spring morning," he said.

Beatrice flushed.

"How's your faithful dog?"

"Immortally sweet and faithful," replied Beatrice.

Jed continued to focus on Beatrice's bodice, to the point that it was making her uncomfortable.

"You know I always wished I'd met you first, before my brother did. You could sense that, couldn't you . . . all those nights the three of us were together? I secretly lusted after you. How could you fail to divine that, Beatrice?"

"Oh, Jed. We mustn't hurt Edgar. It's unfair."

"Everything is fair when lust is concerned. Tomorrow I could be under the sod. Wouldn't you rather travel to eternity knowing two brothers desired you instead of one?"

Beatrice nodded.

There was a sudden knock at the door.

Fred barked.

"Go see who it is," Jed said. "I promise I won't leave.

It was the mailman. A package marked unable to deliver Edgar had sent to Beatrice.

Her earrings and some other jewelry she'd left in an etched glass bowl in the corner cupboard. Among the pieces was a gold watch that had stopped ticking decades earlier. It had belonged to her mother, Alba. Edgar knew she wanted the keepsake.

But here it all came back. Address unknown.

The mailman had a milk bone for Fred. "Where's Fred this morning? I thought I heard him."

"Sleeping under the table," Edgar replied offhandedly.

When he returned to the glass table, Jed had disappeared. Edgar's heart sank. He suddenly realized the mailman had seen him wearing Beatrice's dress.

"Oh Jesus Christ!"

Would the neighbors now begin to gossip? He'd have to be more vigilant. Nobody's business who lived in the house. "Surely the mailman has seen more than he cares to admit. Perhaps he didn't even notice. The Fremonts across the street—now who knows what's going on behind their door?"

Edgar finished the tea but felt saddened.

Why had Jed said what he did? Didn't he know how it would affect him? And why hadn't Edgar guessed it earlier? "I never lusted after his woman," he fumed. "Goddamn it, Jed! How could you betray your brother that way?"

He cried out with such rage that Fred started barking and jumping at the window. The sheers keep getting snagged in his paws.

Soon Fred found a shaft of sunlight on the Heriz carpet and began licking himself. He looked winsome in the Japanese-lantern dress.

* * *

As the days and weeks passed, the neighbors were surprised to see Edgar Giles walking alone on the route he normally strolled with Fred in the morning.

"Something happen to your dog?" one inquired.

"Years have taken their toll on dear Fred. He gets his exercise in the house now, up and down the stairs, in and out of the many rooms." Edgar laughed gleefully. "Yet, this old dog needs to keep moving."

"Of course!" came the cheerful rejoinder.

Edgar appeared such a happy fellow of late. He had a bounce in his step. Not as lugubrious as the neighbors had formerly observed him. He waved to them now. Said good morning more frequently. Didn't appear as pensive as he once had.

"You don't suppose he has a new woman, do you?" one neighbor asked another.

"I've seen no evidence of one."

"Perhaps he is just beginning to realize how much better off he is in Beatrice Giles's absence. God, what a harpy."

"I always felt sorry for the poor man."

"Well, some serendipity has occurred in his life. God willing, we be as lucky."

It was now a full life indeed.

Jed had finally consummated his lust for Beatrice. Fred was eating chicken and steak tips instead of kibble soaked in a tepid broth of tap water. And most satisfying to Edgar were the daily conversations with his father.

Long afternoon conversations like they once enjoyed.

He didn't really mind the Beatrice-Jed mating. Better Jed put up with her than he. Much simpler that way.

There was only one major drawback to this carnival of events for which Edgar was the designated ringmaster.

Nothing saddened him any longer. His loved ones were at his side daily and often late into the evening. Doing myriad duties. He needed nobody. Nothing outside the house. He no longer used the telephone. The mail piled up in the vestibule. Fred continued to bark at outside noises, but Edgar would merely stand a distance away from the windows, staring out the sheers to ascertain who wanted to bother him.

"Please," he muttered. "Just leave us alone."

Then one day, as dawn was breaking, he went into the back yard and knelt at Fred's grave. Barely discernable now. With a pocketknife he sliced the sod open and reached into the shallow grave for the box in which he'd swaddled Fred.

Maggots, hundreds of them, scurried out of the cerecloth and up Edgar's arms. He shuddered, lifting what remained of Fred. It was lighter now and felt like collapsing bones, no longer the firm body of the dog that once resided under the dining room table.

Edgar placed the bones back into the container, kicking dirt back over its lid.

He returned to the house and went upstairs into his closet. He lifted out that same saffron silk dress with Japanese lanterns that Beatrice had worn that day to greet Jed, held it close to his body . . . and felt bones. Like dense crickets they gave off clicking sounds when he squeezed. He let the garment fall to the floor.

He scurried into the basement where years earlier he'd helped his father undress in preparation to bathe in the cellar's shower. It's where his father wept before the water flowed out of the bronze rose, washing them of the time they'd wasted calling each other from distant doorways.

And he recalled when he embraced his naked father . . . how he'd felt bones.

They clicked like jacks tossed across a hardwood floor.

Returning to his living room, Edgar called out to Jed, who appeared in the fiery gladiola in the vase on the Chinese table. He could see his image in the watery glass top. Jed was crying for having betrayed him, for having taken Beatrice in his arms and brought her breasts to his fiery mouth.

"They were dry," he told Edgar, "dry and bitter as quince. And when I lay on top of her . . . I heard her bones tapping against each other like a snare drum's funeral march.

"Like the *second line*, Edgar.

"Beatrice is ahead of the second line.

"Hear the snare drum's tap, *tap, tap, tap*?

"Come follow us, brother.

"Beatrice is waving a lime-green parasol and marching shoeless over the red clay. Our father is behind her, blind, but closely following Beatrice's japonica scent.

"Then me, dear brother. I'm behind him wearing my pinstriped suit with an orange flame billowing out of my suit jacket pocket, my bare feet kicking up the dust to the tune of clicking bones and the *tap, tap, tap* of the snare drum.

"Fred at my heels. Snapping at them, the ornery critter.

"Now you, bringing up the line."

Tap, tap, tap.

Edgar never answered the door.

"Why did you title it 'Lament'?" he asked.

"I was unable to cease grieving my brother's death, even though it happened a decade earlier. From that point in time, I processed most of what occurred in my life through that lens."

"You are Edgar?"

"Yes. And Jed is Jeremiah, the deceased."

"Who is Beatrice? Was she your wife?"

I paused before answering. Why was I being so candid with Eli? What did any of this finally matter to him? Yet I could not betray his nascent trust in me.

"She was a comely young woman my brother and I had both known."

Eli—ostensibly satisfied with my response—uttered, "Oh," and switched off his light.

By this time, I knew to await another query.

"You were lamenting having betrayed your brother?"

In truth I was.

I sat up in bed and laughed. There was enough starlight illuminating the room that I could see my outburst disconcerted him.

"Eli, you must understand by now how writers often revisit those periods of their lives that lie awake in their consciousness and whose pain the passage of time has failed to assuage. But in the retelling, it's as if one is driven to throttle the torment with embellishments and obfuscation.

"Yes, I had been grieving Jeremiah's absence. But I was also ruing having betrayed him while he was alive. I don't know which haunts me more: the loss of our closeness, the sense that half of me died when he did, or the way I abandoned all shame while he was alive.

"When we were boys, he looked up to me because I was several years older. But that changed once he reached puberty, and each of us slept on our respective far sides of the bed.

"Going our own separate ways couldn't occur soon enough.

"But a decade or more passed before we sought each other out. We were both single at the time. We shared a small apartment in Philadelphia and paired off cooking the weekday nights. Neither of us was much interested in the opposite sex and seldom went out except for an occasional dinner on a Saturday evening. On Sundays we took long drives and dreamed aloud of buying a large tract of land in the country where we would build a house with a barn and a workshop.

"Each evening following work, after a couple glasses of wine, we'd begin imagining ourselves many years out, doing the very same things together, sleeping in the same room—separate beds this round—while being judged eccentrics by our neighbors.

"Yet it was one of the happiest periods in my life. He felt the same. There was nothing we wanted for.

"Until he brought the woman in my story home."

Eli, wholly absorbed, was now perched on the side of his bed.

"When she walked in the door, I felt as if we'd met before. Her immediate reaction mirrored mine. While Jeremiah moved skittishly about, anxious as to how I'd respond given that he'd never told me he was seeing someone.

"It seems, prior to our living together, the pair had been lovers, but then separated. Neither explained why, but it was plainly evident that my brother was euphoric over their reconciliation.

"Do you see where this is headed?" I asked.

Eli eyed me dispassionately and muttered: "The betrayal." Yet he appeared to be interested in something more.

"She was at once winsome and guileless, and her presence caused Jeremiah and me to feel abashed for having lived such detached and neutered lives. Despite her being much younger than either of us, she acted as if she were older. We were the ones who behaved like adolescent boys.

"She teased our awkwardness that evening, exposing what had been absent in our lives as her heady laughter aroused our dormant libidos.

"And, prior to her saying goodnight . . . Jeremiah looked crestfallen while standing in the doorway, waiting to drive her home.

"I imagine you are able to fill in the rest, Eli."

He looked to be gathering his thoughts before he spoke: "How long did you see her without your brother knowing?"

"Perhaps days."

"And the dreams you and Jeremiah shared?"

"Died."

"Did he confront you?"

"For killing the house and barn we were going to build . . . or for fucking her?"

I awaited his response. Nothing.

"*Which did I betray, Eli?*"

* * *

Scarcely a week had transpired when Eli confronted me at bedtime: "Who was Black Wine?"

My God, I thought, *he's making connections that never occurred to me.* He was back riffling my stories for clues. To what, at this point, I didn't fully apprehend. I sat up in bed.

"Why do you ask?"

Eli once again began reading.

"Black Wine."

Was she perfume or fermented liquor?

"Are you certain you want me to call you that?"

Her car door slammed shut. She rolled down its window and said, "Yes. Now get your ass in here."

It amuses me when women take the initiative. I never question if I am up to what they might offer. Often, I see it as a kind of bravado and hang loose for when they forget what buttons to push, or how to throttle us out of a nosedive. Men get tired of playing the lead; it becomes tiresome, boring, devoid of sparks. So, when Black Wine told me to hustle my ass inside the rear of her Nash Convertible, I complied. I even leaned back and smoked a Gauloise. As she drove through the Pennsylvania countryside, the ragtop made clothes-on-a-line noises in the brisk night air. Occasionally a gust of wind in the drafty back seat would blow the ash off my cigarette.

"Slow down . . . Black Wine," I said several times.

"Am I going too fast for you?" she asked.

"Turn the radio on," I said.

"Ain't no radio."

"A convertible with no radio!"

"Didn't want no radio," she said.

That beat the hell out of me. We were now accelerating down a dirt road with nothing but dry cornfields on either side.

"Does your mother's washing machine got a radio?"

"Of course not," I said.

"Well, same difference."

Black Wine's Nash Convertible was one of only seven hundred manufactured in America in 1947. By any stretch of the imagination, it was not a machine of utility. My mother was in servitude to the wringer-washing machine. The only thing it did for her was keep her hands aseptically clean and perpetually chapped. Eventually she resorted to churning the clothes in its tub with a chopped-off broom handle. Its yellow paint got eaten away and then the damp wool fibers began to string off its bone. But the Nash Convertible—onyx black, burgundy leather seats, no radio, a horn that approximated an A-flat flugelhorn burst—didn't even insinuate an air of utility. Black Wine was aware that her automobile transcended its destination. The Nash Convertible elevated all things utilitarian, albeit ephemerally, like sex.

"I don't get it," I said.

"Sure's clear to me." she said.

I had ceased smoking. Now we were circling Pymatuning Lake, a good thirty miles beyond Hebron. The ragtop rippled steadily now. She had to raise her voice.

"Your mother sing when she washes clothes?"

"I've never heard my mother sing."

"Lullabies?"

"Maybe she did. Maybe she didn't. I don't remember."

"What's her name?"

"Esther."

"Oh."

"What do you mean, 'Oh'?"

"That's why she didn't sing."

I think I was beginning to catch on. "Where are we going?" I asked.

"Be patient."

Pymatuning Lake Road ran for a good ten miles until it broke off into several small camp lanes that veined up into a range of mountains. A full moon illuminated the lake silver. I had never fished in it, but as a young man I'd swum out fifty yards offshore with a young woman friend. I lowered the bathing suit off her breasts, and we pumped our legs to keep afloat. Nothing more. It was quite serene. Our friends back on shore had no idea. I'd never felt a woman's breasts up close like that. This night with Black Wine I mused on that experience and imagined Esther stirring our clothes in the Maytag as if they were apple butter.

"You don't like the name Esther?" I asked.

"If you are called Esther, you're obliged to clean mud-stained bed sheets and panfry potatoes. Scour scuzzy rings out of bathtubs and toilet bowls. You got to suck dust mites out from under beds and bureaus and vinegar your windows to let the sunshine in. Esthers ain't obliged by ragtops with no radios. Only table pickings and farting, belching husbands."

She finally pulled onto a dirt trail that terminated at a square clapboard shack with no porch, one window, and a door. The threshold stood two feet off the hard soil with no steps. A screen door banged freely against the side of the camp. Black Wine turned to me. "You want a radio?" She laughed and motioned me to follow her into the shack. Hammering against the bottom panel of its door until it growled open, she hoisted herself up. Once inside she ignited a kerosene lantern, then reached down and pulled me in. I shut the door.

"This is Betty's place," she said.

"Oh," I muttered.

The cabin was barely furnished. A one-and-a-half-person cot primly covered by an Indian blanket sat next to a wooden table with two ladder-back chairs. A rodent-eaten, wine-colored, velvet-upholstered easy chair accompanied by a side table holding the kerosene lamp sat against the opposite wall. And over in one corner, a porcelain double sink rested on two cut-off Louisville Slugger bats. No skirt. A small medicine chest hung above it with a mirror whose silver had mostly vanished. You could just gather shards of your face when you stared into it. The source of heat stood in the center of the square room: A kerosene stove-pipe heater, porcelainized Delft blue with chromium trim—shined and brightened like the Nash Convertible. Black Wine lit it. I sat in the easy chair. She lay down on the bed and removed her leather hiking boots that I'd admired earlier. Argyle socks somebody might have knitted brightened the austere room. The walls were painted sanctuary white, adorned by only a single piece of paper tacked alongside the one window. From a distance it looked like a child's scribbling. I rose to study it. The paper, once torn from a composition book and crumpled, read: *To Betty*. Followed by three x's and two o's. It was signed, *B.W.*

Black Wine was still lying on the bed. I turned to her and smiled. She broke into a feathery laugh. "Outside that door," she gestured, "there's an old Kelvinator with rubber wringers sitting on the lawn. You're welcome to turn on the radio if you want."

"What's coming out of it now?" I asked.

"No diapers, that's for sure."

"Overalls?"

"Nope."

"Bed sheets, towels 'n' handkerchiefs?"

"Dirt. A bushel of it and dead snapdragons. Real pretty in July, though."

I watched Black Wine as she took off her jeans and sat up on the bed, leaning against the wall in her panties and a khaki shirt with epaulets and pearl snap buttons. Sterling silver barrettes held back her auburn hair—one near each temple set with cat eyes.

"Reach under your chair," she said. I slid out a one-burner affair and placed it on the table. Canned Sterno—when I pried off its lid with a quarter, its sweet addictive odor perfumed the room. We were going to have tea.

"Where'd you bury her?" I asked as we waited for the water to boil.

She gestured behind her.

I nodded.

"Damn heavy, you know. I couldn't drag her too far. Just didn't have the strength."

"I understand," I said.

"You been to any funerals lately?" she asked.

"No," I said.

"Oh," she replied.

I poured the hot water into two mismatched, chipped china cups.

One said "Coon Chicken Inn"; the other was a piece of speckle ware. Neither of us took sugar. There was no icebox to hold cream.

"When did she pass away?" I sat beside her in the narrow bed, my shoes resting alongside hers on the shiplap floor. Both our backs to the wall. Bringing the cup of liquid to her mouth and before sipping, she relished the steam rising before her nose and eyes like a veil.

"August. One summer ago. Died right here in this room. She was ill for some time before that. We waited as long as we could, then one day she asked me to bring her away from the city. We both knew. We didn't tell anybody and drove here just like you and me did, in the night.

"Waited until morning. The two of us wide awake, just staring. At sunup, I took her outside, we hugged once . . . and she began to walk off out the dooryard and back up into the pine and hemlock. I hung behind her. And then I heard some branches cracking and there was a thump. Like a sack of sand bein' tossed out the back of a pickup.

"I dragged her another hundred yards or so. Kicked some soil onto her face, covered her body with last year's pine needles. I untied her shoes and put them longside her head. Just like she were lyin' in bed. At the ready, like two loaves of nut bread. I knelt on my hands and knees and crossed myself . . . like I've seen the Roman Catholics do. It don't mean nothing to me. But it might mean something to her . . . 'cause she was spiritual. No radio in her washing machine, huh?

"I said a made-up prayer. Some stupid stuff—like:

If you are going on a long trip, Betty,
carry a flask for Jesus
and yourself
and tie bark about both your legs
in case of snake bites
and if your skirt gets snagged
and rent
rip off a piece
tie it in your messy hair like a ribbon.

God likes pretty women, ya know.

And the dirt on your hands and your feet—

don't give it no mind, Betty.
He just going to lay you down anyway.

Deep down where the Shiloh runs shallow and clean.

"Then I came back here. Shoveled soil into the Kelvinator and sowed the snapdragon seeds from a package she'd placed near the basement window back in the city a few years ago. The flowers on the package had all faded. But Jesus, when I returned, they were rising out of the old white porcelain barrel, waving buttery yellow in the morning sun. Weren't a clothesline around. And the air smelled just as clean as springtime. Though it were fall."

Black Wine took off her shirt and lay down on the cot. She curled up into a fetal position and didn't give me any sign that she wanted me to come into bed with her.

"Would you like the blanket over you?" I asked.

She shook her head.

I could hear the wind blowing outside. It beat against the ragtop of her car. Just like there were clothes on a nonexistent line. A large quilt, perhaps, or several sheets slapping against themselves out there in the moonlight.

Eli dropped my journal to the floor and lay back down while staring at the bedroom ceiling. "Black Wine is the very same Beatrice you and Jeremiah knew, isn't she?"

"Yes. But I was unaware of that when I wrote the story."

He grew silent. As I began to connect the two women in my mind, I thought only the author could confirm that they were one and the same. No description in either narrative would attest to this.

Was it because he knew her also?

"What do you know that I don't, Eli?"

"Black Wine," he said, before turning off the light.

Were our narrative worlds—his MacLeish Sq. and mine—beginning to coalesce?

I had to acknowledge there was a strong, perhaps subconscious, association between Black Wine's persona and Jeremiah's lover. Each was proudly independent, an attribute that only heightened my attraction.

I recalled the few times "Beatrice" and I were alone together. One was on a long car trip we took to Montauk where we stayed overnight in a motel. She drove with me alongside in the passenger seat. Wasn't it supposed to be the other way around? We shared a bottle of wine en route while she regaled me with amusing stories. I heartily laughed and coaxed her to continue, thinking how pleasant it was to have a woman take the lead.

Stopping for gas, she returned to the car with coffee and two packs of cigarettes—one for each of us. After we entered our motel room and spotted twin beds, it was "Beatrice" who shoved them together.

When we made love that night, she sensed my preoccupation for having betrayed my brother and whispered:

"Put it out of your mind. It's my choice."

I understood then that Jeremiah and I were expendable. She was going to be attached to nothing. Least of all a man.

The last evening we spent together, I knew we were unlikely to ever meet again. When she put on her coat to leave, I asked her to please stay.

"Why? So that I will forget you?" she replied.

CHAPTER SIX
ELI

I watched her sing these words to the hallway mirror.

He just going to lay you down anyway.
Deep down where the Shiloh runs shallow and clean.

By the time I was old enough to understand, I saw photographs of the person she had buried. In one she was sitting on a porch swing with her mother, each woman in a plain shirtwaist dress and lace-up shoes with anklet stockings. Probably watching for my grandfather to return home from the tin mill. Like time had stopped, I could smell dinner warming on the stove.

But something had happened to her prior to my entering the world.

Early on I learned not to expect a photograph of mother and son on a porch swing, or one of me in my first communion suit, or even a dream image of us riding brightly painted carousel steeds.

Always her unspoken message was: "Find your own way, Eli."

He just going to lay you down anyway.
Deep down where the Shiloh runs shallow and clean.

I recall nights in my room, longing for her to enter and comfort me. Yet I knew the door would never open. Did I think any less of her? She'd found a way to not depend on others. I had to also.

Those men in her life. What fools they were. Couldn't they see what I saw?

Did I love her? It's a word I don't use.

I was Eli.

With no father.

"Look around," she replied. "Pick whichever one you like."

And we'd both laugh.

* * *

I was now certain John Proctor had known her.

For the first time since I'd stood outside his studio window my coming here felt validated.

He and I were now more closely allied than I'd imagined.

Including Jeremiah.

Strangely, I began to experience consecutive dreams of MacLeish Sq.'s annual winter Basilica production of Dante's Second Circle. Each night was a repeat of the one where the lustful are being lashed about in a whirlwind. But in place of Francesca and Paola suffering the punishment were John Proctor and the young woman for whom he betrayed Jeremiah.

At the climax of each dream was the dramatization of those guilty of betrayal in the Ninth Circle . . . their faces frozen in ice, preventing tears of remorse.

> Each face looked down. Their mouths all testified
> to the bitter cold, and all their eyes were signed
> with the depths of misery that gnawed inside.[x]

Without fail I awoke at this moment to sit up and stare at my host in the bed alongside me. The starlight entering our room had lit up his face as if it were cast in ice—the pallor of crystal luminescence.

In Rodin's *La Porte de l'Enfer*, Paola's head of sorrow lingers permanent in the viewer's consciousness.

Yet that face was not mirrored here.

Perhaps it's only in death or art where our transgressions surface in ice relief.

> Early in *Moby-Dick*, Ishmael narrates that a "moody stricken Ahab
> stood before them with a *crucifixion in his face* . . ." [xi]

It's that expression that now traced John Proctor's brow.

Instead of bringing us closer together, the revelation—and to where it might possibly lead—caused him to become wary of me. Except now I had begun to feel guilty, as if I'd darkened his being.

He wished I wasn't in his house, sitting across from him at the dinner table, wandering about his fields as he tried to paint.

The canvas remained bare. John Proctor was now haunted by what I'd dragged in.

Neither of us could have known.

* * *

A paralysis overcame my host and me.

I read and took long walks. Earlier, when he heard the front door open and shut, he would have been at my heels, urging me back.

Now we both knew that no one was leaving.

One morning he asked that I join him at the breakfast table. Fractured small talk commenced until he opened a ledger and began reading to me.

WHAT ABOUT YOUR DA?

The wheel-less fire engine. The naked dames in Dominick's noggin. All kid stuff, Eli.

But I did play the piano. My father, after a few drinks, would stand behind me and sing the popular songs of the day. "Play this one for me, Son." The real maudlin tunes I'd embellish with Liberace arpeggios, provoking laughter in his voice, although I couldn't see him. But I could whiff the whiskey.

One night when he was under the weather, bellowing out "Poinciana," he called Mama from the kitchen and asked her to accompany him. She shook her head in disgust. "Well, dance for us then," he insisted. "Like you once did when we were first married. This very table you used to dance around. Please, Rose."

Except she would have none of it.

It was like the piano was nothing but a cast-iron harp strung with wires and lowered inside a tomb of walnut. I could hear the air whooshing out of my old man who was still standing behind me.

It's why I had to move to someplace where I could live with all the characters in my head, my real friends who never disappoint me.

But Christ, do I ever miss the crooner. I'd fantasize us going from saloon to saloon stoking up the quaffers' melancholia. I never wanted it to end. 'Cause when it did, it always turned dark and forbidding. You understand what I mean?

I mean the old man had to go to bed to get up for work the next morning. Mama would stick a bologna sandwich with a fucking orange into a paper sack for him, day in and day out through all eternity. Her standing there in an embroidered apron mechanically buttering the white bread and slathering it with mustard. Like the kitchen clock was mocking us as it ticked away boredom.

Nothing ever moved in the house. The dining table frozen in the same spot for years. As was the Formica dinette in our kitchen. I could have been blind, and I'd know where every piece of furniture was and what drawers in my bureau held my socks, underwear, the shirts I'd wear to school.

I'd get the same sack lunch as my father. When I'd head out for school, I was so brought down by the experience I'd return home late afternoon and want to fall into bed, close my eyes, and try to think happy thoughts. 'Cause they'd all been hijacked by having to sit the entire day, listening to teachers who I swear climbed out of their graves each morning and prepared their sack lunches before coming to class with scribbling on what could have been fucking papyrus. When they opened their notebooks to begin teaching, Jesus, all I could envision was the slugs they'd transported from their loam graves crawling out and down their arms. Trying to escape just like Dominick wanted to.

Then soon I'd hear my old man walk through the front door and collapse onto the sofa. He'd sigh just like I would when I entered. Then you'd hear the pans being banged down on the gas stove in the kitchen and Mama scraping around in her slippers preparing supper. I'd want to scream: *"Why are you feeding the fucking dead! Haven't we suffered enough?"*

You get what I'm saying?

The American Songbook . . . he knew them all. Memorizing the melodies on the car radio on his way to the factory.

Pretending Mama was one of those dames in the tunes he was warbling for.

Except Mama had given up.

And what hurts me most of all, Eli, is how in Christname my old man ever gets on in the afterworld. How often can you warble yourself to sleep?

With me at least he could pretend we were a saloon act. Father and son. That we were on the road romancing all those long-limbed porcelain beauties.

He made my heart sing.

What about your Da?

He closed his ledger, slid his chair away from the table, smiled and headed to his studio. I didn't see him again until bedtime. He had his reading light on with that very ledger open.

And I sat up in bed because I imagined John Proctor sitting in the chair at my bedside sipping cognac. A full moon cast a swath across the right side of his body . . . illuminating a portion of his white shirt, black tie, and blazer, which he hadn't removed at dinner. The cognac glass appeared full to its brim with amber light. His face in the shadows as were his lower extremities.

"*What about your Da?*" he asked.

"Oh, mine never sang," I said.

I turned away from him, facing the wall.

He switched his light off.

I could hear him stirring in his bed. Minutes passed interrupted by a car horn outside.

"Eli?"

I didn't respond.

"I have a woman down inside me. Like you, Eli, I think."

I froze.

"I could hear her breathing at night when I was all of six years old. In my dreams she'd put her moist lips to my eyes like compresses. First one eye and then the other. At times when I was most fearful of one thing or another, she'd dip her tongue into them. It felt like a wet hibiscus petal. And when that happened, I could detect the odor of that hibiscus as if it were rising out from under the sheets.

"There were nights she would dance nude alongside my bed. Sometimes she was an old woman with dugs like ice buckets, milk pails strung from her shoulders. At other times she was a prepubescent girl with fuzz at her groin and breasts that were but a suggestion with faint purple haloes.

"And sometimes she'd say, *It's just me, John. No, it's just you.* And then laugh, as if the joke was on both of us. Upon seeing that I was confused or disturbed, she'd lie flat on me, her face to mine, her torso to mine, her thighs and feet to mine, and tightly grab hold of me like we were about to go for a very fast ride. Maybe over the water on a speedboat, or down a snowy slope on a sled, or fly by ourselves over the white birch trees outside our house."

He turned to face me, knowing our eyes would meet.

Something I'd never seen him do, he took a quaff of the bourbon he'd placed on the stand opposite the window side of his bed.

"It's what I wonder to this day, Eli. *Did she become me? Because of some fear I had of becoming her?*

"So, what do you say to that, Sassafras?"

Of course, he didn't wait for an answer. John Proctor switched off his light.

"I understand fear," I said.

"No, that's not what I want to tell you, son. What I mean to say is that I wanted to write stories like the one I just told you, on the faces of others. I wanted to see how they answered the questions that I haven't been able to answer for myself.

"But you know what the biggest question was?

"Think about it, Eli.

"We're each of us lost in an unrequited love affair with that person down inside ourselves.

"Da never had anything to do with it.

"*Who do you think he caroled those love songs for?*"

* * *

How was I to interpret his message?

As I lay there reflecting on the Da story and then his response to it . . . how could I understand it other than John Proctor's baring his soul to me?

Revealing his inability to be anything other than a storyteller about people who yearned and had feelings for others where he was void of the capacity.

Each of us had come perilously close to having to reach out, make a commitment.

And even he had to put that truth in an aphorism.

"How does the soul bare itself if all it has ever known are words?"

Yet John Proctor had put all that behind him . . . or so he thought. But now in the person of myself, *it* was lying in a bed opposite his and breathing the same air. He believed I shadowed him with every step I took.

His inviting me in now threatened to unmask what he was never able to reconcile. And he still did not know what that was.

I had become John Proctor's bane.

Long before daybreak, upon affirming he had fallen asleep, I abandoned our room and penned a note to him:

Da, I'll catch up with you in MacLeish Sq.

Queequeg's life-buoy lay on my bed.

CHAPTER SEVEN
JOHN PROCTOR

"Consider all this; and then turn to this green, gentle, and most docile earth; consider them both, the sea and the land; and do you not find a strange analogy to something in yourself? For as this appalling ocean surrounds the verdant land, so in the soul of man there lies one insular Tahiti, full of peace and joy, but encompassed by all the horrors of the half-known life. God keep thee! Push not off from that isle, thou canst never return!"[xii]

Eli had underlined the above in the copy of *Moby-Dick* that lay open on his desk. His "Tahiti" was MacLeish Sq., and he was headed back.

It was Queequeg who saved Tashtego from being buried alive in the whale's head, recounted by Melville as an act of midwifery.

Had I not taken it upon myself to give birth to Eli of no-name?

Also, I thought about Starbuck in the blackness of a roiling sea igniting a lamp and handing it to Queequeg.

"As the standard bearer of this forlorn hope. There, then, he sat holding the imbecile candle in the heart of the mighty forlornness. There, then, he sat, the sign and symbol of a man without faith, holding up hope in the midst of despair."[xiii]

And Ishmael's view of the universe as a "vast practical joke."

Was not the lamp that I held up for Eli in truth for me?

"From the pallor of the dead we borrow the expressive hue of the shroud in which we wrap them."[xiv]

Even the community to which I had returned, when I wandered through it at dusk, I saw only what I called back. The ardor long since drained from my memories. *Pale horse Pale rider.* Even the unearthly thunder at night no longer frightened me. The hours crept by like cats. Nothing bothered me, for then I had to be somebody I no longer was.

Dead and loving it.

In the quiescent light at bedtime, I sang softly to my breath. She had kept me alive so that I could die and continue to waft the musk of night air. Perish and be awakened by a lover's sigh.

Perhaps Eli was still too young to see all that. How long had he been standing there observing me prior to my seeing him? I couldn't say. But knowing the young man as I now did, he surely perceived I was wearing white: the pallor of the dead.

I gestured that he come in. Now I was destined to follow him.

Shadowing him to MacLeish Sq.

And for all I knew, it was somewhere in my past.

* * *

There existed a ledger of my stories and unfinished novel excerpts that Eli had no access to. I'd purposely stored it out of his and my sight because it touched a time in my life I was loath to revisit. A sentient reader would understand why.

THE EFFIGY

"When he first appeared . . . I'd no idea who he was. I was performing in summer stock in Pittsburgh. This was early on before I settled in New York City. The plays were the usual quotidian workhorses and I had begun asking if this was what I wanted to do the rest of my life. One August evening after the show, I borrowed a friend's car, filled it up with gas, and began driving. I didn't know where. I simply wanted to get away from it all, try to clear my head. The season would soon end, and I wasn't interested in signing on for an Our Town tour through the Midwest.

"You've been in that kind of space, Christopher. You know what I'm saying.

"So, I'm traveling through West Virginia a couple hours later and about to go over this very high and long trestle bridge. I've always been leery of heights and I get particularly nervous when I must cross a bridge in a car or on foot. Well, this one had jelly-jar lamps that glowed an insect-green lining its parapets and which I found particularly magnetic. I'm traversing the bridge slowly when I see a figure waving to me from the railing.

"*He's flagging me down*, I think. But when I slow down to stop, he disappears. At he's leapt off the bridge. I stop the car, jump out, and run to the railing. Except I can see nothing in the skylight but the river coursing far below. Also, there is no sign of a car parked or any clothing left behind.

"I climb back into my friend's car and decide that I should turn around and head back. That this may have been an omen. I'm rather spooked by it.

"Recrossing the bridge, I purposely keep my focus straight ahead, refraining from even studying the parapets and their green, glimmering, jelly-jar lights. I begin to grow less anxious when it's long behind me.

"Several minutes later, I light a cigarette and a voice alongside asks if I have an extra.

"Startled, I turn to the passenger side, and there, wearing a wry grin, sits the person I saw hailing me from the trestle bridge's railing. He raises his hand as if to assure me there's no cause for alarm.

"'How did you get in here?' I ask.

"'When you jumped out to peer over the railing,' he says.

"'What's happened to you?' I ask. 'Is there something wrong? Has your car broken down or what?'

"'Nothing's wrong,' he says. 'Say, how about that smoke? No, I often walk this route at night and I'm especially attracted to the bridge that you cross. It seems I always end up crossing it halfway and then staring down, far down, into the river . . . wondering if I have guts enough to take the plunge. It draws me like a magnet. So many nights I find myself testing myself to see if I have what it takes to draw back from the magnetic pull. And then I feel whole again. Like

I can make it through another week or so. That nothing is going to get to me. Do you know what I mean?'

"I say that I do.

"Then he asks if I'd mind if he turns the radio on. He wants to find some music. 'Any kind,' he says. As if that moment when he waved me down was particularly distressing to him. That perhaps he was about to give into the pull. That this could have been the night.

"Frank Sinatra is crooning "As Time Goes By," and the stranger sits quietly smoking while barely humming the melody.

"'Where are you going?' I ask. 'I mean where do you want me to drop you off.'

"He doesn't answer.

"The next Sinatra tune is 'In the Wee Small Hours of the Morning.'

"'Is he one of your favorites?' I ask.

"No response.

"I turn to look at him and it's at that moment, Christopher, that I begin to get it. The stranger sitting alongside is me. I mean the only difference between us is that I'm driving the car and he isn't. Each of us is smoking and watching the roadway pass under us.

"He turns to me and says, 'What would you like to talk about? Personally, I'd prefer listening to some more Sinatra.' And we both laugh.

"'Why now?' I ask.

"It's as if he wishes to ignore me or didn't hear what I said.

"'Why have I not seen you before?' I ask. 'Why are you coming out to me now?'

"'You weren't prepared for me. You need me now where you didn't earlier.' He gestures with a wave of his hand to the bridge, now miles behind us. 'It could have been you standing there at the railing, right? Except it was me. Really you, Ethan. But me.

"'It's how we are going to get through this . . . with each other.'

"That was his first appearance, Christopher. Frankly, it all seemed quite normal. I wasn't disturbed by it. Actually, I found it intriguing and somewhat comforting. As if life had suddenly taken on an extra dimension.

"Mile upon mile we traveled that evening without a word between us. Each of us was caught up in listening to more Sinatra tunes. Then they played a full hour of Billie Holliday. We went through a half pack of smokes. When I was headed back through the Liberty Tubes and into Pittsburgh's downtown, I turned to inquire what happened next. I mean I was curious as to how we'd proceed.

"But the passenger side was empty.

"No sign of him.

"As if none of it had taken place."

"How do you know you weren't hallucinating that night, Ethan?"

"Hallucinations don't smoke. Furthermore, he looked just like me. Or a mirror image."

"How soon after the bridge incident did he reappear?" I asked.

"Only in the direst of circumstances."

"You mean . . ."

"When death threatened. Independent of whether I was fully cognizant of it or not."

"It was you who contemplated jumping off the bridge, wasn't it? And not the stranger."

"Yes. He saved me more than once. Strange, wouldn't you say? Did he want to live more than I? That's what I keep asking myself. For if I went back . . . he would by necessity follow.

"So, I'm certain he, my real other self, merely kept in the background until circumstances necessitated his appearance.

"But it was not always so apparent."

"I don't understand. What do you mean?"

"One night in a Belgian hotel he shows up at my bedside. I am with a woman and couldn't have been in better health and spirits.

"Having arrived with others in my theater company from the States earlier that week, I had gone through customs dressed as a Roman Catholic priest. Many of us in the troupe were periodically using LSD and hashish. It was simply another role for me—I relished testing myself as to how well I could pull it off. I mean carrying the stuff on me.

"Others in the company had begun to expect such risky behavior from me, and I frankly enjoyed not letting them down. They knew

I was up for just about any damn thing. I simply didn't give a shit about much, Christopher. That's who I was then.

"So, a couple nights later, following a performance and minutes after having made love to some lovely who had hung around after the show . . . I'm lying next to her, enjoying a smoke and happen to glance over and there sitting in a chair is . . . yes, that so-called stranger. He's dressed exactly as I had been days earlier—as a priest. A black suit with a clerical collar. Reflexively I look to see if the young woman has noticed him. She hasn't. I mean he is only there for me.

"I try to ignore his presence because of what it represents. Yet, I'm having difficulty processing it because I'm in fine fettle. I mean the performances are going well, the intelligentsia are sweet on us, and we're acting before sold-out audiences wherever we appear throughout Europe. I want to cry out . . . *'What the fuck are you doing here?'*

"She wants to make love again and this fucking priest, my masquerade, is queering the mood. I simply can't get him out of my head. The girl wonders what she's done wrong. I assure her not a damn thing. That it's my fault. Something simply popped up in my head that I've no control over.

"I turn away from her, hoping the apparition will go away.

"Instead, he stands up, wanders over to me, and begins to cross himself, assuming a very serious mien as if giving me absolution. Then I realize he's giving me last rites. I bound out of bed.

"'No fucking way!' I holler.

"She's now sitting up and bed totally spooked and says she'd better leave.

"I try to tell her everything is okay . . . it's my overactive mind. But now it's all too late and she's putting on her clothes and saying goodbye.

"When she closes the door, he's standing there observing me with an expression of total empathy.

"'What is it?' I cry. 'Why are you doing this to me?'

"He sits back down and looks away.

"'What are you holding back?' I persist.

"And then it happened, Christopher. A metamorphosis right before my eyes. It isn't the phony priest, me, sitting there. *It is my father.*

And he's wearing this silly grin like he had fooled me. Like it was him all the time. That he's the real actor and not me.

"He reaches out his hand to me . . . says he wants me to come back home. That he has no one to sing to. That Momma doesn't love him like I did. That when he stands at the piano, he feels cold. Because I'm not there. There are no shoulders he can put his hands on. No ears he can croon into.

"'Come home, Son,' he says. 'I miss our rides. I miss listening to the radio in the dark car with you. The yellow headlights shining our path in the pitch black and the little red light on the dashboard from where all the music emanates. That magic. You and me, father and son. Come back home, boy.

"'Let's Get Lost.'

"I'm so moved that I go over to him, get on my knees, and reach to take his hands in mine . . . except they are cold, Christopher.

"Ice cold.

"Like they would never thaw.

"I look up at his face. The mist in his eyes had frozen.

"He looks straight ahead, right through me.

"It was then I knew."

I began to ask myself what my real motive was in stopping Eli from heeding the voice inside . . . the one he claimed was his father summoning him home.

Was it for his sake . . . or mine? Because I knew where *home* was.

"There, then, he sat, the sign and symbol of a man without faith, holding up hope in the midst of despair."

Did I not want Eli to experience what I had when I was his age? Or was I fearful of being drawn back into that vortex where the voice had beguiled its presence back to me?

I now believe it was both.

It was as if Eli had carried the ague back into my living quarters. For decades, I had endeavored to bury the memory.

Perhaps Eli's sudden appearance on my doorstep was the presaging the voice had returned.

It was one thing to fear I'd once had an intimate relationship with his mother. Quite another to think he and I shared a diabolical "Father" from Hell.

As if someone had entered the house and left the door open, I felt a sudden chill. Except it was early May and the red tulips had opened to the sun in my garden.

Was Eli the newest guise of my double, even more accursed?

Was he, in truth, the voice summoning me home?

One touch and the gossamer separating reality from madness dissolves like a moth's diaphanous wing. A mark of ash on my forehead.

The double is always brighter and more compelling than the lamp of the persona it mirrors. Not unlike Proteus, it has the capacity to assume many identities, each with an authenticity equal to Yahweh's.

And in these moments, I felt I was succumbing.

> *Now amid the green, life-restless loom of that Arsacidean wood, the great, white, worshipped skeleton lay lounging—a gigantic idler! Yet, as the ever-woven verdant warp and woof intermixed and hummed around him, the mighty idler seemed the cunning weaver; himself all woven over with the vines: every month assuming greener, fresher verdure; but himself a skeleton. Life folded Death. Death trellised Life; the grim god wived with youthful Life, and begat him curly-headed glories.*[xv]

"The greatest mystery of all is reality."

Yet another metaphor that came racing forward in my consciousness, one flaked in dry humor, was that of Ahab's ivory stub hole that kept him firmly anchored on the *Pequod's* deck. I'd now slipped out of mine.

Looking about my surroundings, I began laughing at what I'd led myself to believe had become a sanctuary. My studio . . . the chapel within. What did any of it mean now that the past which I could not escape had entered, forgot to shut the door, and sat down before me?

CHAPTER EIGHT
ELI

My Return to MacLeish Sq.
Part I

To my surprise no one deigned to recognize me.

When I approached Ishmael, even he stared at me quizzically.

"But I am Eli," I protested. "Your star acolyte. Don't you recall?"

"I'd prefer not to," he replied.

Then as if to shed a sliver of light on my dilemma, he gestured to the Basilica's cast door, a crude replica of Rodin's *La Porte d'Enfer*.

"Behold the phantoms groping about there in a futile attempt to recreate their lives on earth. Have you come back to MacLeish Sq. in a vain effort to recreate who you once were?

"Join those 'others' who roam about peddling their stories, praying that one of us will be so moved as to grant them an identity. If lucky enough, you too can become who you no longer are."

And that evening, sitting alongside the embryonic statue of Hawthorne, I recalled from my childhood how my mother longed to join Jesus Christ. It was always at night when we were alone in the house. Knowing that she would be abandoning me, I asked why. "To make a place for us," she said. "You will have somebody who knows and loves you when you arrive, Eli. Could we pray for anything more?"

In the utter stillness of the square, I felt saddened by how she had deluded herself.

There was no Heaven. For life's but a preview of its perfidy.

And even if there were, like the Basilica portal, it would be populated by phantoms seeking in vain to reenact their estranged lives on earth.

In those dark hours I prayed for Eli to reappear so I wouldn't feel so utterly lost.

Before the women in gray locked the sanctuary's doors at midnight, I climbed the stairs to the balcony and occupied a pew closest to the railing overlooking the nave. Flickering candles illuminated its side chapels.

As I lay there, I heard a stirring below and sat up to observe one of the homeless women attired in a white homespun nightdress. She ascended the pulpit, placed a lit candle on the lectern, and began singing as if she were the soloist leading into the sermon . . . except no sounds came forth.

I was unable to tell how many others were looking on from the deep shadows of the sanctuary. No starlight penetrated the stained-glass windows.

Having spent countless nights—especially early on—finding my sleeping quarters there, I wasn't surprised by the sight. The indigent often enacted out their dreaming. And given that the Basilica had once been a house of worship, it was not unusual for their sleepwalking to exhibit religious overtones. This night the "parishioner" in white sang from an imagined hymnal.

A second women in similar attire soon approached the pulpit stairs followed by yet a third. Now the mute choir, with perfervid conviction, held forth before those slumbering in the pews beneath them.

It dawned on me that I had encountered the trio at Hester Alley's harbor entrance. Their self-appointed station in life was to greet and offer directions to those armada passengers stepping onto shore. Always dressed in white, each affected a ghostly presence, particularly on an overcast and misty day.

Were they sisters?

The women emoted with a prayerful repose, suggesting neither joy nor despair, which I construed as an unsettling paean to fate.

I stifled the urge to cry out, "I can't hear you!"

When they snuffed out the candle and lingered motionless in the stygian air, I imagined them a tableau vivant of the three shades at the apex of *La Porte d'Enfer*, about to acclaim: "*Abandon hope all ye who enter here.*"

It was at that discrete moment I experienced an insight that profoundly impacted my senses . . . the sanctuary's stained-glass window biblical figures burst to life in effulgent sunlight.

Rushing back down into the Basilica's atrium, I ran out into MacLeish Sq.

My God! I cried. *I have been set free.*

Eli wasn't real!

He'd been fabricated over the years by how others perceived him and his forlorn longing for their approval. Was he not doomed like all those slumbering inside the sanctuary?

My time with John Proctor, craving to win his acceptance, gazing wistfully into the tranquil interior of his painting studio . . . Who was I looking for?

Eli, of course. But Eli who? . . . My absent mother's? My ghost father's? Why was I slave to an identity I didn't own?

I relished the irony of my racing out of the Basilica feeling resurrected.

Hours earlier I'd wept for Eli's return.

Before three shades sang a mute's lament.

Once while perusing John Proctor's art books, I'd become captivated by Rodin's *non finito* sculpture *La Pensée* of his lover and pupil Camille Claudel's head. Resting atop a roughhewn block of marble, her face with polished flesh is tilted forward as if in buried reverie. "*Emblematic,*" the caption read, "*of the struggle of man to free the spirit from matter.*"

And in these awakening moments I more accurately grasped my condition, savoring breath in a manner that heretofore had eluded me.

I'd found Eli.

The more I came to confront this truth, my primary concern became:

How to bury him?
The paradox I found bitterly amusing.
Do I lay him to rest, or let those for whose approval he yearned do it?
Except I no longer had a choice.
Their affirmations had grown cold.

* * *

The morning following my night in the Basilica, I wandered about MacLeish Sq. as one who had been born again. I bristle at using that term, but I can explain my feelings no other way.

My major test of course would be confronting Ishmael again. For MacLeish Sq. was, if nothing else, a redoubt for those who sought recognition. To be condemned as an *other*, a *no-name*, in the square was an insufferable prospect for most.

Yet now I had become one and never felt freer in my life.

> *"I (Ishmael) felt a melting in me. No more my splintered heart and mad-dened hand redeemed it. There he (Queequeg) sat, his very indiffer-ence speaking a nature in which there lurked no civilized hypocrisies and bland deceits . . . I'll try a pagan friend, thought I, since Christian kindness has proved but hollow courtesy."*
>
> *"He pressed his forehead against mine, clasped me round the waist, and said that henceforth we were married; meaning, in his country's phrase, that we were bosom friends; he would gladly die for me, if need should be."[xvi]*

Two of the myriad *Moby-Dick* passages I had copied into my journal.

It was Queequeg's flame of "utter serenity; content with his own companionship; always equal to himself" that beguiled me. The pagan's indifference to others "speaking a nature in which there lurked no civilized hypocrisies and bland deceits."

These passages could only release their unvarnished truth to a ready mind.

Ishmael—who presumably was considered "saved" because of his Christian faith—is freeborn by Queequeg.

I now perceived their "marriage" in a fresh light. Henceforth I would strive to be always equal to myself.

* * *

Being a persona non grata in MacLeish Sq., I now ventured to regions on its periphery. I'd been told about the river Phlegethon—so named because of its red rapids—that during a spell of insufferable heat and airless sunny days, its waters took on the appearance of blood. Some residents swore that it in fact was blood, and God's reminder of the community's wickedness perpetrated during the witch trials. Others, whose imaginations were more benign, professed it to be runoff from the tannery mills bordering its shores. Notwithstanding, the river was considered off limits by most residents.

The Wood of Suicides that lay on the waterway's banks added to the enigma of Naumkeag's darker perimeters. Its name, of course, like the Phlegethon's, was derived from Dante's *Inferno*. For, whoever committed suicide, their souls were cast by King Minos into Hell's seventh circle designated for those who did violence against themselves. There they grew into gnarled bushes or trees to be tormented by Harpies—bird-like creatures with women's heads—who ripped off their leaves and branches.

The suicides perpetually cry out.

As a child I chose not to explore the area. Rumor had it that every month or so a denizen of the square disappeared into the Wood. Most hanged themselves from the trees. Despondent others would reside for several days among the dense oak, hickory, and maple prior to committing the act. On deathly hot summer nights, one could hear the afflicteds' keening. Christmas day the choir of the depressed became most pronounced.

It was not uncommon for the community's more pious adults to threaten an obstreperous child with banishment to the Singing

Trees: a hell more real and terrifying than that heard described from the Sunday pulpit.

The late spring afternoon I chose to wander through the Wood, the skies were overcast, and the leaves had begun to create a nascent canopy. An occasional shaft of sunlight would escape the cumulus sky, causing me to ignore the dire attributes of the glade. In fact, it was quite lovely and the customary sulfurous odor of the river was absent. I chose to expunge from my consciousness thoughts of the lost souls who had entered there to perish.

It caused me to wonder if the Wood by its very reputation had lured several inside.

Likewise, to consider that not long ago this might be the very place to which my father had summoned me.

Yet I was not by fear possessed. And as the shadows began to lengthen, I was about to retrace my steps and head back to the square when there—several yards ahead, standing with his back to me—I spied Ishmael in his black robe.

I froze, hoping he would wander out of view.

Except he wasn't moving either.

In his thunderous ministerial voice, he cried out: *"Where is she?"*

I dared not respond.

"You, I'm asking." Ishmael swung around and pointed directly at me. *"Where is she? Or have the singing tress seduced your presence here as they have mine?"*

"I don't understand what you are asking of me," I replied.

"This place is not unfamiliar to her . . . surely you know that, Eli."

He elongated the syllables of my name while approaching me.

"Nobody has seen her for several days. Or aren't you privy to that?"

The tone was one of condescension. And spite. The source for either remained a mystery to me, particularly given the high esteem I'd previously accorded him.

I had no desire to reply and turned away, hurrying my pace out of the Wood.

Ishmael called out: *"Eli, your mother has disappeared!"*

I didn't answer.

He cried out twice again. The words ricocheted through the Singing Trees.

That evening I visited the Falling Man. The barstool she normally occupied was empty. The tavern was unduly quiet, and the anticipated choreographed forte between a few regulars and the bartender never occurred. If I hadn't experienced the exchange that afternoon with Ishmael in the Wood, I might have attributed the silence to a communal rebuke of my presence.

But now it became apparent that many besides him were concerned over her absence. My last encounter with her replayed with vivid relief in my consciousness:

Secure within herself, nursing a drink, and conversing with no one on either side of her. A nightly presence in black wool and a tightly gathered hair bun. Except her right hand she now cradled in her lap, out of sight. Only when she raised her glass did the amber liquid tremor.

I had not given it further thought.

Then I recalled Ishmael's prophetic insight:

"*She was who she wished to be that night and who they desired to touch, however virginally, as they circled the* Souls of the Dead Dining Room. *But lust beat life into their atrophied hearts. How they wished to ravish her in those secret chambers. And she goddamned well knew it. And that, my dear son, is why she danced with them. That, dear friend, is why our male hearts beat on her time.*

"*Remove her and we revert to birdsong.*"

I wandered back out into the square. It appeared abandoned. Even the benches alongside Nathaniel's statue were vacant. For as long as I could recall, at least one of the Ishmaels milled about even late into the night as if they had agreed among themselves that one had to be "on call," especially for those who wandered up Hester Alley, having been newly dropped ashore from the ghostly armada.

The Cotton Mather was equally subdued. Its unoccupied sofas and chairs in the waiting room evoked an eerie furniture refuge. A lone receptionist watched my every move.

What revved my feelings of unease was hearing the august

Bösendorfer in the *Souls of the Dead Dining Room*. Glancing in, I witnessed Charon playing "Every Time We Say Goodbye." Yet no one was seated at any of the tables. Not even a waiter stood in attendance. Nor was the pianist attired in his customary tuxedo with oversized lacquered lapels. Instead, he was attired in an Ishmael robe. Upon finishing the tune, he performed it again. Then again.

I felt an impending sense of dread.

Is that why I had ventured to the Singing Trees that afternoon?

Too cowardly to head into one of Naumkeag's side streets to seek her residence, I headed back to the Basilica.

To my utter surprise, it was lit like a High Holy Day celebration was taking place inside. At this hour of the night the indigents would normally begin to straggle in.

As if expecting me, the ladies in gray smocks met me in the atrium. One opened the door to the narthex.

There, high up in the sanctuary's apse, was the fully illuminated rood . . . only Christ's flesh radiated the texture and appearance of ice as if His body were composed of frozen water. Its frost-white illumination cast a spectral pallor over the occupied pews.

I climbed the stairs to the balcony and sat looking out over those below.

They gave the impression of waiting for a performance to begin.

At that moment I spied Ishmael exit his side chapel and advance to the pulpit, where he extended both arms to the buttressed ceiling and clerestory.

The illumination in the ice-Christ began to dim.

Ishmael's sonorous voice caused the grand stained-glass windows lining the basilica to hum as if he had placed his bulbous lips on each to create the dissonance.

It was an unsettling sound.

And then I understood the purpose of this night.

Ishmael had evoked our childhood memory of the Singing Trees.

Some in the audience didn't understand. They were strangers to the Wood of Suicides. But others visibly shuddered in the pews. Muffled sobs broke out.

Ishmael didn't relent, standing there rigidly like a statue, his mouth wide open, intoning one unnerving note.

But it wasn't he.

He was merely the masque.

For I witnessed filing into the choir loft three women dressed in white, the Shades of this Service, keening the single unceasing note of unbearable grief.

The carolers had immortalized the cry of each who had who entered the Wood alone.

Several in the audience abandoned their seats and rushed back up the nave to exit.

One grief-stricken woman stood and cried, "Esther!"

Did Ishmael believe the suicides would reappear?

Yet they had no bodies to claim, having abandoned them in the glade of trees alongside the banks of the Phlegethon.

Then it struck me: Who was he calling back? Was this a communal seance to summon she whom he sought early that afternoon?

The Basilica grew dead silent.

Ishmael hadn't moved from the spot, his arms still extended as if in benediction to the heavens.

The pew occupants froze as if having absorbed the ice of the Lord's body shining down upon them.

To me it seemed an eternity.

Only then did Ishmael cry out:

"*HAVE YOU SEEN HER?*"

Once again to the vaulted ceilings:

"*I SAY, HAVE YOU SEEN HER?*"

The burn in his voice palpable.

Fearful that he, summoning me forward, would exclaim, "ELI," I prostrated myself and crawled to the balcony steps. Within moments I was back outside.

From the Hawthorne statue's vantage point, I watched the Basilica's doors open. Holding aloft a lantern I presumed not unlike that which Starbuck thrust into Queequeg's hands, Ishmael strode forth followed by the three carolers. They were accompanied several paces back by the "parishioners" bearing votive candles in an array of clear, crimson, and gentian-violet glass containers. The solemn procession advanced in the direction of the Phlegethon and the Singing Trees.

Ishmael's expression of one obsessed caused to flash in my mind Hawthorne's Black Man of the Woods in *The Scarlet Letter*:

> *"How he haunts this forest, and carries a book with him,—a big, heavy book, with iron clasps; and how this ugly Black Man offers his book and an iron pen to everybody that meets him here among the trees; and they are to write their names with their own blood, And then he set his mark on their bosoms!" Pearl asks: "Didst thou ever meet the Black Man, Mother? . . . And dost thou go to meet him in the nighttime?"* [xvii]

I shadowed the throng out of MacLeish Sq. toward the river. A half-moon effected an icy overcast on the water. As they moved along its banks toward the Wood, the flickering votive candles suggested fireflies, a swarm of them in the thrall of a bright amber glow emanating from the lantern now suspended high from Ishmael's scepter.

Within minutes, the Wood of the Suicides quivered with light.

Outside I waited for Ishmael to summon her presence.

Instead, there was no sound.

I saw only the votive lights scurrying among the trees in a demoniac frenzy, but the illumination from Ishmael's lantern, held aloft, never stirred. I envisioned his acolytes being swept about the trees by a violent wind. Yet there was no sound to indicate that or even an audible buzzing.

Deadly silence.

Until the votive lights, not unlike a ring around Saturn, returned to cluster about the lantern's amber glow.

As if in a moment of quiescence.

Then it came . . . the high-pitched lament that had induced the Basilica's stained-glass windows to shudder.

A keen so penetrating that it froze the soul.

Amid this aria, the votive lights scurried haphazardly throughout the Wood.

The spirits of the suicides taking flight.

Only Ishmael's amber lantern light shone motionless.

The piercing sound ceased.

Exiting the Wood one by one, each votive-candle holder walked separately back toward the Sq. Only after they'd disappeared did I see the lantern light extinguish and Ishmael reappear, dressed in street clothes. The black cloak, scepter, and unlit lantern he carried by his side.

I chose to hang back and considered entering the Wood.

Did I think I'd meet her there?

Like the embers of a waning fire, a haunting murmur caused the Wood to seem alive. As if Ishmael and his entourage had awakened those who had sought peace within its embrace. I feared who—or *what*—I might encounter among the singing trees, for she had often talked about "going to another place."

Had she called it Heaven so as not to terrify me? Is that the way despondent mothers broach the truth?

Instead, I walked away. At an earlier time, I would have been unable to resist running headlong into my worst fears, convincing myself I'd find her there . . . and then be forced to witness her anguish.

"Yes, I lied to you, Eli. I've been drawn to these woods since I was a child. Couldn't you tell? Who would not dream of entering the woods where the trees weep?"

The Basilica looked dark when I climbed its front steps. But when I entered, a lady in gray appeared and handed me a blanket, like those other nights I'd taken refuge within its walls.

* * *

An hour or so after turning in, I heard a stirring and spied Ishmael exit his side chapel in street attire and pad toward the exit. I quickly dressed and was soon following him at a safe distance down Hester Alley. Was he meeting someone at the harbor? He turned up a side street and headed toward the run-down residences lining Gallows Hill. I knew the neighborhood well, having once lived there.

He must have detected my presence. Could he have turned into one of those doorways? Was he watching me?

Approaching the tenement where I'd last visited my mother several years earlier, I looked for signs of him. It was a house in disrepair with a foyer leading into a dark hallway off which there was a tenancy on either side with adjoining bedrooms up a narrow staircase.

Did I dare try the door to her rooms? Or once again was I about to give in to the draw of the *invisible world* that was so much a part of MacLeish Sq. and its environs?

As I was about to return to the cobblestone pathway, Ishmael stepped out of common reeds surrounding the house.

"Don't you want to go in and see her?"

He'd startled me.

"Are you fearful of what you might see?"

I shook my head.

"Then come."

Ishmael chortled like he would when I visited him at the Stove Boat.

"It's just as well," he said. "For her room is empty. There is no sign of her."

"Then why do you return?" I asked.

Ishmael passed by me and prior to picking up his pace, he turned.

"Some of us can't leave, Eli . . . as you did."

Why couldn't they leave? I wondered.

I saw nothing to prevent any one of the MacLeish Sq. inhabitants from departing.

A fatalism of sorts betrayed his and others undisguised contempt for my having left and returned.

I was no longer one of them.

My current situation I found highly amusing. It was as if they, including my Ishmael, were all grasping onto Queequeg's casket like their lives depended upon it.

The mortal fear that *she* had abandoned them.

Now I was a vestige without an identity. Not unlike one of the shades, having been dropped off by the armada out in Naumkeag

Harbor and walking up Hester Alley seeking to be heard, recognized, and christened anew.

"The Charles Bridge" was one of John Proctor's stories I'd carried with me because I could never fully understand it, and yet the narrative had intrigued me, for it was my introduction to Gregor Samsa.[5]

Upon returning to my bench in the Basilica's balcony that night, I returned to this passage:

> *A parody. Every day of my life. But I had nobody to speak it to save for a few close friends. Late afternoons and evenings the script filled more notebooks. They piled up, collecting dust under my bed, on various surfaces in Old Town, and outside the castle walls on Golden Lane. I dressed each morning in proper attire and conducted myself in society as if there were nothing so grotesquely mad to laugh at. Often when I crossed the Charles Bridge, staring down at the silvery Vltava, I wished to dissolve myself and the history of my race into its icy swell.*
>
> *There was no succor. Except the farce, that is. Who I was and those about me. Who we are under our garments, behind the velvet curtain. The theater in my belfry was what sustained me. The little plays I would act in and entertain myself with alone at night in my study.*

Struck by how presciently the words limned my predicament, I couldn't help but wonder if they had done the same for my host. Was the Charles Bridge-cognizance what had been stalking John Proctor's life? Is this why he escaped to the burg of his youth to live out the remainder of his life happily estranged from himself?

Until I intruded, accosting him in his painting studio?

The irony that our relationship was perchance forged out of a shared odyssey and not brokered with blood caused me to erupt in laughter.

In the belfry's theatre . . . paternity pales.

---

5 Gregor Samsa, fictional character, an overworked salesman whose transformation is the subject of Franz Kafka's symbolic novella *The Metamorphosis*.

Awaiting sleep above the cicada of snorers in the pews below, I felt light in spirit and comforted by calling back John Proctor. He had crossed the Charles Bridge before me.

Therein lay our bond.

My Return to MacLeish Sq.
Part II

Having read and reread *The Scarlet Letter*, I could hardly underestimate the abiding influence and presence in Naumkeag of the long-deceased Increase and Cotton Mather. Its narrator opines:

> "I seem to have a stronger claim to a residence here on account of this grave, bearded, sable-decked, and steeple-crowned progenitor—who came so early with his Bible and his sword—he was a soldier, legislator, judge; he was a ruler in the Church, he had all the Puritanic traits, both good and bad. . . . His son, too, inherited the prosecuting spirit and made himself so conspicuous in the martyrdom of the witches . . ."[xviii]

The spirit of the father and son had after hundreds of years never fully vacated MacLeish Sq. Indeed, the Cotton Mather Hotel with its *Souls of the Dead Dining Room* was merely one of numerous establishments attesting to their legacy.

> *"The scarlet letter had the effect of the cross on a nun's bosom."*[xix]

Cotton and his hanging justices dancing with her in the hotel's dining room, is that not what grew lucent in each of their souls . . . a fiery amulet on her flesh-white breast?

But it was the insidious potency of their grave influence that concerned me now.

"All the Puritanic traits, both good and bad."

My encounter in the Wood of Suicides with Ishmael and his acolytes exhorting me to reveal "Her" where abouts bore a striking resemblance to Hawthorne's common superstition of the Black Man:

"who haunts this forest and carries a book with him—a big heavy book with iron clasps; and how this ugly Black Man offers the book and iron pen to everybody that meets him here among the trees; and they are to write their names with their own blood. And then he sets his mark on their bosom. . . . And it glows like a red flame when thou meetest him at midnight, here in the dark wood." [xx]

How could Cotton and his black-cloaked assemblage not desire to dance with "Her"? Those passionless ledgers of death and Biblical denial, papyrus men, driven to suckle the imagined breast that once nurtured them alive. Their obsession with a woman's flesh, the odor of birth and procreation, the red mist of concupiscence.

It was at this moment Charon appeared and took his place at the piano. The gentleman at the head of the table, one I recalled as Cotton Mather, it was he who stood and faced Charon.

"Please, Maestro, a melody for this wondrous occasion."

. . . When Reverend Mather had finished, each of the other gentlemen took their wooden turns. Not one broke a smile, not one touched any part of her body except her hand, nor betrayed the suggestion that he detected the scent of musk rising from her person . . . or theirs.

Even Charon dared not cast a wistful glance in her direction.

* * *

Those new ghost-armada arrivals. Their expressed need to be christened with a new identity. How, obsequious, they would follow in the shadow of any one of the Ishmaels, often trying out a character they hoped might catch the tutor's attention. For without an Ishmael's sanction, they remained the "others."

How curious, I thought. It was the black-cloaked Ishmaels who authenticated the identities of the MacLeish Sq. occupants. For they were the acknowledged learned ones, the scribes who had committed whole texts to memory, the veritable libraries of the square. Perhaps it was different in some other place. But here, Hawthorne, Melville, Dante, and to a lesser extent Poe, held sway.

I recall thinking how weightless the "others" appeared to be, darting from one gathering to another, hoping to be acknowledged by a gesture of recognition, or perhaps even a warm smile. But they were without ballast.

To me they appeared as *nether* men and women. Like they'd arrived from some unknown place seeking a reason for being alive.

The Ishmaels were their only hope, for they were the keepers of the Ledgers within which each "other" prayed that one day his or her name would be so inscribed.

For one young man I endeavored to help assuage his despondency. "But you have a story," I urged. "You came from somewhere, and you are alive. What is yours?"

He shook his head. "No. That isn't my story. It belongs to somebody else."

"How can it not be yours?" I asked.

"It's a hand-me-down," he said. "As if an old hag had sewed me together. Claptrap here, a bit of the Bible there, good citizenship thrown in, somebody's anger and hatred that I caught like diphtheria . . . and it's all stitched up into me. You'd run away from that too.

"I'm screaming inside that 'other.' Can't you tell? I want to get out."

Of course, back then I couldn't fully grasp what he was intimating.

It was as if they had crawled back from Hell to redeem themselves by becoming somebody they never were.

I couldn't erase the mental image of the "others" about the square bearing their dead souls inside.

Not wanting to be identified with their ghosts, they rarely changed their stories.

Even in the depths of night they would flit through the streets and alleyways.

And why here? Why MacLeish Sq.?

Was it not the very same reason why I had found my identity here? Had not the Melville tutor, my Ishmael, sanctified Eli? Except I arrived as a boy. Whereas the "others" were grown men and women.

And what better place to exist than within narratives already transcribed by the sons of New England? Tales that had already been consecrated. The "others" fortunate enough to become acolytes of the Ishmaels were no longer condemned to look back upon their pasts and shudder.

They found redemption in the side chapels of the Basilica and acceptance in the daily colloquies in and around Hawthorne's statue.

Within months of receiving an Ishmael's nod of recognition, each moved about the square less burdened.

They were no longer themselves.

But now I too was an *other*.

Moreover, the Eli that I carried within me had, from the beginning, been nurtured by the square and Ishmael, conversant in its literature, and able to recite passages from *Moby-Dick* long into darkness. I was raised on Bartleby and Billy Budd.[6] Chillingworth was not the next town, and Dimmesdale could have been my father in another life. I've yet to catch his scent or share our birthmarks. Young Goodman Brown might be my double.

Charon, my ferryman.

I can name the longest rivers in the world, including all those coursing through Hell. King Minos's query to the damned, "Who comes into my house of pain?" is as memorable to me as old Fleece's sermon to the sharks. And I'm more *au fait* with Ahab than Job, and less inclined to envisage God than Queequeg's coffin that may save me.

I dressed each morning in proper attire and conducted myself in society as if there were nothing so grotesquely mad to laugh at.[7]

It was a suit very similar to the Joseph Beuys felt suit I once saw in a photograph.

Except mine had not been destroyed by moths. I also wore a felt homburg with a black grosgrain hatband like that of the Germans.

How could I not be inspired by an artist who made a piano, then covered it in felt so that it could never be heard or played . . .

---

6 "Bartleby the Scrivener" and "Billy Budd": Short stories by Herman Melville.

7 "Charles Bridge" excerpt by John Proctor, pp 104.

but evoked the expectancy of sound? Or upon visiting the United States wrapped himself in heavy felt and wandered about with a coyote, his sole companion. "I wanted to isolate myself, insulate myself, and see nothing of America other than the coyote."

John Proctor had inadvertently introduced me to Beuys in one of his many art books.

Even encountering my former tutor, Ishmael, in the square and knowing he would refuse to acknowledge my presence, I was able to insulate myself from the sting by envisioning the felt-swaddled upright.

Who could inflict anguish upon what they couldn't see?

At the break of daylight, I'd don a white dress shirt stiffened with starch and a purple tie, crawl into the felt suit, check the rake of my homburg in my pocket mirror then descend the Basilica's balcony steps to the outside world.

A peripatetic piano swathed in felt.

Rarely a day would pass that I wasn't amused by passing an earlier acquaintance who would begin to gesture a greeting before he caught himself and moved on. It was in that momentary meeting of eyes when I signaled he might press one of my keys. I'd gladly unfurl the felt.

"If you only knew," I thought. *"Eli's dead, but look who has shown up in his stead."*

When frequenting the Falling Man after dusk, I could no longer sit at or near the bar.

Besides, it didn't matter. After a couple of weeks, I no longer missed Eli. Others did perhaps, but not me. I found it so much more interesting listening to and studying the square's denizens than I had when feeling obliged to converse and associate with them. I was much happier inside the metaphorical upright where all my strings were more or less in tune.

I firmly believed somebody would eventually condescend to inquire what lay under the felt . . . then play me.

Yet despite my general wellbeing, it had been several weeks with no sign of my mother.

She was the reason why I visited the tavern most evenings, trusting she might appear. But even those patrons who had known her well stared blankly when I inquired into her whereabouts.

Did they think she was dead?

The encounter with Ishmael and the acolytes in the Wood of Suicides led me to believe that she could very well have taken her own life.

Still, I sought hope in the unspoken covenant we shared: each owed the other a last goodbye.

"When I least expect it, she will appear," I kept telling myself.

Would she recognize me in my felt suit?

CHAPTER NINE
JOHN PROCTOR

I have come to believe that the whole world is an enigma, a harmless enigma that is made terrible by our own mad attempt to interpret it as though it had an underlying truth. —Umberto Eco

Bathing in a nightmarish world of light and darkness, for thirteen days—I counted them—I rarely ate and mostly lay on the couch in my studio shrouded by a white sheet. The phone had been lifted off its cradle. At intervals I'd imagine Eli sitting across from me on the floor telling me of his return to MacLeish Sq. and would catch myself laughing or crying. Yet I didn't want him to stop.

For it was my only encounter with reality . . . such as it was.

I was terrified that he might leave, for then it would be only me in the room.

And when it became evident that Eli was gone, I berated myself.

Please leave too, I said. *Can't you see we have nothing in common? Could you bear my calling you a sycophant or something worse? Pusillanimous, perhaps?*

But I could see this stranger standing before me picking his teeth with a red toothpick and smirking.

Who are you? I wondered.

I gestured for him to walk across the room so I might study his stride.

Yes. Now step alongside me, and with the index finger of your right hand trace the outlines of my face, beginning at the forehead.

He hesitated.

What? You're afraid of touching me?

He warily moved so close to me that I imagined his breath on my face.

With eyes closed, I awaited his touch and sensed his anguished hesitation.

The finger crossed my forehead horizontally then dipped into the hollows of my eye sockets, before humorously skiing off my nose then lingering for infinity on my lips . . . or so it felt.

There, I said. *Please settle down here alongside me. Let us be friends, for there are no others.*

The eve of the thirteenth day is upon us.

I'll sing you to sleep.

At the break of dawn, I awoke feeling whole again. The long night had passed, it seemed. I opened all the windows in my study.

For reasons I couldn't fully interpret, I dressed myself in white. In my closet hung an alabaster linen suit I'd worn decades earlier as a young man, having purchased it on a whim upon meeting a woman I was attracted to. It had been a chance encounter on the street. I'd mistaken her for someone else. Or so I told her and myself.

And white shoes.

I had to find Eli.

Prior to closing the house that morning, I returned to my study and considered removing the shroud from the standing easel. Then thought better of it. Perhaps during those many long hours and days of hallucinations I'd captured the image of the adult male simpering at me, a red toothpick between his lips.

"*Gustav Aschenbach?*"[8] I inquired.

* * *

From the beginning of my relationship with Eli, I'd always assumed Naumkeag was a mythical place in New England. But I

---

8 Gustav Aschenbach, protagonist of Thomas Mann's *Death in Venice*.

never doubted that it was as authentic as the very self that stared back at him each morning in the mirror.

My immediate problem was finding the town.

I settled on New Bedford, using *Moby-Dick* as my guide. Recalling the Spouter Inn where Ishmael and Queequeg first met prior to their sailing off in the *Pequod*, and knowing Eli's fascination with the South Sea native, I convinced myself we'd meet there.

But after several days of milling about the town and environs, I gave up and traveled north to Salem, for where else might I find Hester Alley and the Cotton Mather Hotel?

My first evening there, and several yards from my lodging's entrance, I encountered a realistic bronze casting of Nathaniel Hawthorne. Within walking distance at the harbor, I spied the Custom House where the author once labored, and farther down Derby Street the setting for his novel, *The House of Seven Gables*.

Feeling passably euphoric, I made a stop in several taverns before turning in that night. Unable to fall asleep—and having imbibed too heartily—I lay there imagining which watering hole most closely resembled the Falling Man. The patrons of those closest to the harbor struck me as regulars, given their convivial repartee with each other and the bartenders. Also, I felt myself a distinct outsider in such establishments, and rightly so.

Before succumbing to Morpheus—though I didn't understand under what circumstances or when—I now believed I was about to make good on Eli's offer to join him.

* * *

Following a week of wandering about the town, I began to register that my sartorial guise had captured the attention of others. There was the occasional nod of recognition in a restaurant or on the street. The white linen two-piece had become appropriately rumpled by now. I even appeared a trifle seedy, conceivably even debauched, which delighted me.

Why should I be concerned if nobody notes my presence?

I wasn't at all surprised when I was approached by a stranger in a bookstore on Derby Place. "Where are you from?" he inquired. "I believe we might have met?" I had been leafing through a history of the witch trials. I looked up to see a gentleman perhaps a dozen years my junior with red hair and flushed cheeks. He was attired conservatively in the manner, say, of a presiding official of the district court jurisdiction.

I grinned and stared at the man, thinking that his approach was an auspicious prelude to my being led into Eli's mythical world.

"It was in a novel, was it not?" he continued.

"Ah, yes," I said. "But in a different locale."

"You won't find him here," he countered.

"It's not he I'm after."

"Oh, then perhaps you will join me in a toast to Gustav."

Stephen Tritos, a Salem jurist, had me follow him down a side street where we entered a doorway marked by a nondescript sign that read *The Black Whale*. Inside was a well-appointed bar and a dining area with cabriole-legged tables and Windsor chairs. The Black bartender was costumed in the tradition of the early train porters, while the clientele was attired similarly to Tritos. Several of them greeted him as we took a table off in the corner.

"Judges and lawyers with an occasional accommodating clerk," he obliged as I looked about, gratified to be in his company as he was my first genuine social encounter since arriving.

"So, if you are not looking for Tadzio,[9] why have you come to Venice?"

"A bit ironic," I replied, "but my reason for being here had its genesis in a similar delusion . . . except it's not mine."

Stephen and I amiably chatted for the next hour or so over drinks. I did share with him my reason for visiting Salem and a brief history of my time living with Eli. Presumably because he specialized in wills and trusts, my atypical yarn aroused his curiosity.

---

9 Thomas Mann's novella *Death in Venice* is about a man's obsession with a fourteen-year-old boy named Tadzio.

"What does this young man look like? Describe him for me the best you can. What are his likes? Who might his friends be?"

Amid my answering, Stephen interrupted.

"Does he sing perchance?"

We locked eyes.

What the hell does that mean? I wondered.

"Permit me to explain," he said. "Yes, I labor in boilerplate law and estate planning, but perhaps by now you gather that I have another side. Just as I'm certain that you have a very interesting one also, John Proctor.

"My life begins to brighten once I depart my dreary office. You see, I am a pianist of a persuasion who performs selections from the American song book several nights a week in the formal dining room of Salem's oldest hotel. Under an assumed name, of course."

Without thinking, I sputtered, "*Charon?*"

Stephen glanced at me quizzically.

"An imaginary friend of Eli's," I tried to explain, but was now overcome by the knowledge that I was on the verge of strolling up Hester Alley. I signaled the bartender for another round of drinks. Stephen didn't protest.

"So why did you ask me if Eli sang?"

"Well, as you might imagine, it's not unusual for a diner to approach me at the grand Bosendorfer, requesting a tune. I always oblige. On occasion one will ask if they might warble. Frankly, I do my best to discourage it. 'We're not a piano bar, you understand?'

"But one evening this past year, there was a group of six at a table near me and in the middle of a favorite ballad of mine, I heard this young man's friends urge him to accompany me. Noticeably embarrassed, he relented and sang in the most beguiling yet vulnerable voice I've ever encountered.

"The diners at the surrounding tables were equally moved. It was as if the young man was channeling the lament of one no longer present.

"I had to take a break when he finished."

Stephen was not at all stunned by my recalling the recording.

By now he surmised he too had encountered Eli in his immediate past.

"Have you seen him since that evening?" I asked.

We had unexpectedly become self-conscious, as if Eli had sat down alongside us.

"No," he answered, shaking his head.

Before departing, I told him where I was staying—a rooming house close to the harbor—while he invited me to visit him one evening in the hotel's dining room.

"I won't embarrass you in song," I promised.

A ghostly smirk curled across his mien.

That evening, pondering my encounter in the Black Whale, I couldn't resist thinking I was hearing "Haunted Heart" playing in an adjoining room, for Eli often played the Jo Stafford recording in his room come dusk. The melancholy it aroused became so over-powering at times that I would go outside for air. It was as if she were lying next to him in bed, singing. Over and over, he'd return the needle on the black shellac.

The young man's inexplicable lament on such evenings perme-ated our house like a late-summer's amber haze shrouds a meadow.

The question now became, when would Eli appear? Word would surely get to him that I'd arrived.

I also knew that MacLeish Sq. didn't exist.

He would take me there.

* * *

Scouring my memory of his bedtime narratives, I tried to convince myself that I was encountering the places and characters he'd refer-enced. Yet each night, alone in my room, I began to question if I'd embellished my recall, given that I was no longer in touch with the young man who said he was my son.

Was I seeking him or myself?

Wandering Salem's streets long after dark, mainly frequenting taverns closest to the harbor, I'd become preoccupied with answering this question, for I believed that being honest with oneself was a prerequisite for entering MacLeish Sq.

After several nights obsessing over this quandary, I became anxious about my own physical wellbeing. I'd stopped eating regularly and no longer cared about my appearance.

When I passed Stephen coming out of the hotel late one night following his set, he gave no indication that we knew each other. So as not to embarrass the man, I looked on.

* * *

Was it my begrimed and now yellowing linen suit that first attracted her? The white shoes covered in suet? I'd ceased catching the eyes of people that I passed. Always, like a child, I studied the cracks in the sidewalk.

She asked for a light.

The line sounds so authentic, it's farcical, I laughed to myself.

Stopping and glancing up, I observed a mid-to-late-forties woman shrouded in black. I could only make out the porcelain hue of her face. Even the lips lacked color.

"I'm sorry," I said. "I don't smoke."

She steadfastly glared at me as if endeavoring to arouse a memory.

I was about to move on when a white-gloved hand emerged from under her shawl and grasped my arm.

"John Proctor."

I recognized the piercing eyes. Otherwise, the scourge of a punishing life and alcohol had blighted the countenance of the young woman whose indelible presence had once provoked an unrequited ache in my being: "*Why? So that I will forget you?*"

It was in that very moment I understood why I should never have sought out Eli.

She had risen from the burial yard of sins each of us commit, and I was about to have to answer for mine.

I glanced down at my suit while brushing back my hair, feigning embarrassment for being caught in this condition.

"*How often I've thought of you,*" I muttered.

Her expression was pellucid, for she had known men like me most of her adult life. Even in her present state she evinced an inviolable dignity, despite the many lovers whose callused hands still smoldered from the intoxicating . . . contours of her body.

"How is your brother?" she asked.

"Jeremiah's dead," I answered.

Whenever asked to respond to this question, I impulsively feel the need to recite the entire litany surrounding his passing as if in doing so I might make the lingering hurt abate another degree.

"He ran through a hayfield aflame, flapping his arms as if they were a crow's wings. There was a window alongside the bed we shared as kids. When the full moon ignited the glass, he'd fantasize about raising the sash and soaring out our back yard to follow the creek back up into the countryside."

"The fire?"

"Poured gasoline into the carburetor of his stalled vehicle—lit a cigarette. Never made a sound. When they brought him to the hospital, I asked how long he intended to keep running. 'Until I fell,' he replied.

"At night I sometimes see him from my bedroom window—like an incandescent trail of ash arching across the black sky."

Caught up in revisiting the memory, I hadn't noticed that she had walked several steps away and was holding her hand up to silence me.

"I have something to tell you," she said.

Fearful of asking what it might be, I thought it best that we cease talking. She was according me that option. As if to say: "*Before this evening, John Proctor, I was merely someone in your past. We can leave it that way—your choice.*"

I was thinking about turning away, leaving Salem, and heading back to my house and studio when I witnessed her abashedly shroud her right hand under the shawl. I recalled Eli's description of her sitting alone at the Falling Man while nursing a drink, its amber liquid trembling.

"Tell me he's still alive," I said.

As if she had been awaiting my question. "Why do you suppose Eli had you follow him here?"

"I can only venture a guess."

"Please."

"Someone told him I could be his father."

"That was me. *Except I was looking for mine.*"

Nonplused, I glared at her.

"You were briefly married when you were a young man, right?"

"It was a mistake on each of our parts," I said.

"No children, correct?"

"None."

It was only upon witnessing her wry grin that I felt the damp ocean air clot about me.

"Sara Phipps chose not to tell you she was with child when you left. Likewise, she only revealed your identity to me in her final hours.

"Don't you recall those few days we spent together nearly two decades ago? I swore it was as if we had known each other at some time in the past. Why was I so attracted to you, John Proctor . . . a man much older than myself. *Why?*"

Repulsed by her inference, I felt my chest constrict.

"Is this a tale your mother told you on her death bed? Christ, shall we begin to count how many John Proctors reside in New England alone!"

"You miss my intention. It's only the story that's worth salvaging, correct? Like your brother flying out the moon-lit window. That's all I wished to share with you.

"I have no claim on you. Just as my mother felt she didn't.

"But Eli is still young. That's why you are here. And, yes, he's very much alive.

"One week from tonight let us meet here, same time. I'll take you to him."

Returning to my room in stygian darkness, I felt as it was *she* who had ferried me across the Acheron. For hours, sleep evaded me.

What if Eli's mother was my daughter?

"You miss my intention. It's only the story that's worth salvaging, correct? Like your brother flying out the moon-lit window. That's all I wished to share with you."

How does one even consider the possibility?

I scoured my memory to see if there was any shared similarity in her facial expression to the person I was once cursorily betrothed. I found none. Especially the eye color of each woman. My former wife's were slate blue whereas hers were gray . . . or so it seemed.

Would I in utter fear of having committed incest repudiate the very existence of the woman who awoke Jeremiah's and my comatose libidos? Can one irrefutably deny something that might have occurred?

Or do such narratives write themselves?

Eli's mother and I were at a loss to explain them.

CHAPTER TEN
ELI

She'd placed a record on her turntable.

"Eli, dance for me."

As I whirled about the room in giddy delight, Leah would light a cigarette and laugh.

Smoked after coitus, too.

Yet it was she who brought them home in her shadow.

What was the attraction?

As it grew closer to midnight, I'd on occasion wander along the Phlegethon's sylvan border, thinking I might confront her there. One had to traverse it to enter the Wood of Suicides.

"Perhaps we'll build a cottage there one day, Eli. Just for you and me."

And one of those nights, just as I was about to cross back over the river, off in the woods I heard . . .

"*Dance for me, Eli?*"

A dog barking in the distance responded.

I began walking in the direction of her voice.

Before long, the forest canopy had obliterated the skylight, and I could barely see an arm's length in front of me.

"*There's no reason to be afraid*," she said.

Several yards from where I stood, I saw her, or was it an apparition? Night enveloping us, only her face and the white gloves were visible. Sable covered the rest of her. The gloves pulsed as did her head, the tremor I'd detected earlier in the Falling Man.

"We come here to get away, Eli, and don't inquire of each other's lives."

"*We*, Mother?"

She laughed. "Oh, it's much too early for you, my son. The theatre only opens after dark."

"Theatre?"

"Don't you remember? How we used to play when you were a child? We would dress up in imaginary clothes to 'go to the theatre.' But we never knew where it was. And you would invent the places where we might discover it.

"'Oh, it's behind the couch!' you'd exclaim. 'Oh, no, I know, Mama. It's in Toledo tonight.' And you'd dance about our two rooms. 'Toledo tonight, Mama. Can we go together to Toledo? Just you and me?'"

"*Mother, please come home,*" I murmured.

At that moment, her white-gloved hands began to flutter about her face, virtually obliterating it.

"You must never utter that word here again. *Home* is what the harpies screech at us each dusk. Having eaten that notion from our souls, they taunt us mercilessly."

She stepped back out of view.

"I must leave now. The theatre is about to begin. Where did you say it might be showing? *Toledo, you say?*"

A small chorus of laughter arose from deep in the woods.

"There. Did you hear, Eli? That should put your mind to ease."

Then nothing.

It was the coursing of the Phlegethon that directed me back to starlight.

One afternoon, days later, while wandering down Hester Alley, I came upon a man with a deformed arm who was handing out flyers, a yellow dog resting at his feet. I tried ignoring him, but he pressed one into my hand.

THE THEATRE OF TOLEDO
Naumkeag's World Famous Production
Tonight on the Phlegethon!

A buzz began to circulate in the vicinity, as many who had taken the flyer began asking, "But where?"

The leafleteer merely shrugged.

"Are you going?" a young girl inquired.

"He's mute," another explained. "Lives upstairs from us."

By late afternoon, a large crowd had gathered at the harbor, holding their flyers as if they were tickets to the mysterious event.

"But what time does it begin?" "Will we get seats?" "Are you sure there will be enough?" "Who's the star?" "Will there be music?"

Once twilight set in, the crowd's anticipation had swelled to such a high degree that at any moment it seemed the harbor itself would mysteriously morph into a grand stage with entertainers in bedazzling costumes.

"Look!" someone shouted, and all heads turned in unison to the leafleteer, who had reappeared.

"Has it been called off?" another cried.

"It's been canceled. I well know it. What else could you expect?" a disgruntled woman proclaimed, tossing her flyer to the ground and wandering back up to the square. Yet nobody shadowed her, especially since the leafleteer waited alongside the others.

It's a non sequitur, I thought.

And just as the bells in the Basilica struck seven o'clock, none other than Ishmael in his robes, followed by his bevy of black-garbed acolytes, came tramping down Hester Alley in single file.

The gathered uttered a joyful, "Oh!"

But instead of joining them, he turned at the corner and headed toward the Phlegethon.

"Of course, Ishmael would know!" a voice rose from the crowd as it moved like an amoeba to the rear of the acolytes.

I followed at a distance.

The procession became solemn at the river.

At a natural clearing—an amphitheater of sorts—the garbed

Basilica throng occupied the higher ground while the others sat cross-legged at the Phlegethon's banks. All gazed across to the Wood of Suicides.

As if on cue, Ishmael stood and singled out the leafleteer, guiding him to stand at the water's edge.

Momentarily we saw on the opposite bank what appeared in the inky black to be disembodied hands in fashion gloves and several women's faces flitting among the trees like white caterpillars . . .

An ethereal choreography.

A woman attired in chalk swaddling and a womb-red military riding jacket emerged from the dark canopy, dragging a long, narrow box. Walking to the water's edge, she called out to the mute leafleteer. Acknowledging her, he opened his mouth to cry out.

Yet all that we heard was the gurgling Phlegethon.

She turned her back to him.

The disembodied gloves and countenances commenced to assist her into the pine craft, whereupon they launched it into the river.

We watched it lurch sideways as if to disgorge the woman before settling into the Phlegethon's swift current.

A flurry of the *Theatre of Toledo* flyers rose out of the open bier to trail in its wake.

I interpreted what I was witnessing as a portrayal of Queequeg's coffin.

The Toledo Theatre's analogical flight from its closing vortex.

> When I reached it, it had subsided to a creamy pool. Round and round, then, and ever contracting towards the button-like black bubble at the axis of that slowly wheeling circle, like another Ixion I did revolve. Till, gaining that vital centre, the black bubble upward burst; and now, liberated by reason of its cunning spring, and, owing to its great buoyancy, rising with great force, the coffin life-buoy shot lengthwise from the sea, fell over, and floated by my side.[xxi]

I couldn't resist recalling my very own fascination with the "coffin life-buoy" when I was being summoned to return "home" by my assumed father. What could save me except a metaphor whose power to seduce the imagination equaled the "wheeling circle's"?

That evening as I wandered back to my room, exalted by the encounter, I passed en route several others who like myself still clung to their flyers, approximating those who exited the grand *Porte d'Enfer* Basilica doors on a Sunday morning, clutching programs for the coming week.

Would the Phlegethon be so foreboding to the inhabitants of MacLeish Sq. now that the Toledo Theatre had entered their consciousness? And what of those who had lost a loved one to the Wood of Suicides? Would that place of no return lose its power to sting?

As these questions flurried about in my head, I had some trepidation about falling asleep, for fear of what dreams might surface. I felt as if a large burden had been lifted from me and believed that I was no longer anxious about the voice returning—gifted with an inner peace I had only experienced as a young boy. Yet something gravely dark hovered over me like a veil, and I feared that once I shut my eyes it would open to reveal something I would be unable to bear.

So, I sat on the sofa reading a newspaper, the contents of which I had already perused. But soon found I couldn't keep awake and fell asleep.

As I feared, I saw my father. *Yes,* I thought, *there is no way you could be denied your insidious power over me.* I began weeping like I'd lost the battle. The *Theatre of Toledo* had been nothing more than a farce to distract me from something that could never change. Who was I kidding? The Wood of Suicides was precisely that: people went there to call it quits. The self-inflicted violence to their bodies was no equal to what they suffered inside their heads.

In a moment of abject defeat, I lay back and waited. *Go on, say it,* I pled. *Let's get this over with.*

He stood there motionless, his countenance one of profound sadness, yet he said nothing. It was then I saw flames ripple up his body and travel out his arms, which, rising from his sides, began to flap as if they were wings.

Neither of us moved.

Just the two of us. One trying to escape, the other wanting to reach out and embrace . . . but was terrified of fire.

* * *

When I awoke, only one thought entered my consciousness:

Perhaps the *Theatre of Toledo* was her way of saying, "Eli, please forgive me."

Of course. I followed her there. As a child.

As an adult, her flyer in my hand.

Where else could it be but to the very same home my putative father summoned me toward?

It was always where she wished to escape.

A wood more persuasive than her paramours.

"Please dance for me, Eli."

This little light of mine.

CHAPTER ELEVEN

JOHN PROCTOR

In Eli's absence I grew anguished over whether I had begun to romanticize how close we had become. Replaying those many nights where we traded stories, some invented out of a need or perhaps even to test the other's authenticity.

In truth what was most difficult for me was that I found myself desiring, nay, *longing* for his affection. Such feelings were new to me. Even the hint that they *might be real* heightened my fear of losing him.

I had so profoundly identified as Eli's father.

How could I brook his leaving me for another?

At that admission, caustic laughter boiled up within me. *John Proctor, you, desiring to be loved? After all those years when you deemed it a sign of weakness?*

Or was I nothing more than an aging man whose life was behind him, living out his allotted days and hours, unprepared to venture into the dark night without another calling out his name?

One's memory of him lying stillborn in a house of empty rooms.

* * *

I waited nearly an hour at the designated spot, but she hadn't shown.

About to return to my room, I heard her voice summon me into the darkness. I could barely see her, even her white gloves, for as earlier she was adorned in black garments. I caught glimpses of her from the back and not her face.

"Where are we going?" I asked.

"Follow me."

Before long we were walking along a riverbank, the water so pitch black that it didn't reflect the little starlight that existed this night.

All along the path, an abundance of common reeds at times rose to the height of each of us. Yet it was an unobstructed path that had been tramped often.

At a clearing she requested that I wait as she fell out of sight.

Across the waterway I thought I saw a flurry of outsized albino moths—knowing no other way to describe them—flying randomly under the canopy of trees.

Then emerging out of the dark wood, I saw only her face, suspended in the air, staring back across the water at me.

"Call him home, John Proctor."

Fearful of what she was suggesting in this tenebrous place, I said, "I can't. One should never summon a son home."

"Why?"

"Because of what he may discover."

"You would not beckon the boy as he felt his father had."

"Now call him."

As the swirl of white moths increased, I uttered his name.

Within moments her face along with the etiolated ghosts vanished from the Wood of Suicides.

Only Eli and I stood facing each other, separated by the tenebrous river.

"Can you come over?" I asked.

"To where?"

"Our place. Where there are no ashen insects outside the windows or voices from other rooms."

He wore the identical outfit that he had departed in, very much like when he first peered into my studio window. Except he was noticeably older now.

"I'll cross over," he gestured down river as if he'd known the way.

I waited in the very spot where she, his mother, had called for me to follow her.

When he appeared, Eli smiled warmly.

"I wasn't certain you would come," he said.

* * *

I couldn't help but believe that this night had been foreordained by Eli's preoccupation with Dante's *Wood of Suicides* but also Hawthorne's *The Scarlet Letter*, specifically Pearl and Hester's foray into the forest.

Not dissimilar to how Queequeg's life-buoy became a talisman for him.

All that he read, the images that inflamed his fierce imagination.

My encounter alongside the Phlegethon that night had been the young man and his mother's narrative. Yet, even then, a part of *my* story was unveiled to me.

As I walked behind Eli back to MacLeish Sq., I did not engage him in conversation. I wasn't yet convinced that what I was experiencing was real. I didn't want to break the yarn's spell. It was enough that I tread in his shadow.

We entered the Basilica and climbed the steps to his pew in the balcony. He handed me a rolled-up garment and gestured that I use if for a pillow. We lay down at opposite ends of the church bench, our feet nearly touching.

No blanched moths in the nave or choir loft.

It felt as if we were back in the bedroom we once shared.

But I divined that Eli was not yet prepared to abandon MacLeish Sq., a place he knew better than any other.

And this night she helped me understand why.

It had been our very own forest walk. Where but there could we begin to return to ourselves . . .

But in Ishmael's house at the crest of Hester Alley, only steps away from the Falling Man.

* * *

As we exited the Basilica the following morning, Eli asked if I wished to experience the veritable MacLeish Sq.

"I assume that's why you came?" he asked.

"My presence here should attest to that, Eli. It was not my home."

With that, he gestured that I should accompany him, and for hours I followed him through his "imaginary" world, as if he were my tour guide.

I: Netherland

As we trod north of the Sq., we came upon a walking bridge Eli named the Charles and the coursing waters below it, the Acheron.

"On the other side exists Netherland, or the *invisible world*. It's the site of Golgotha Hill, where nineteen men and women were once hanged and another crushed to death with heavy stones, Giles Cory. Several inhabitants of the Sq. call it their home."

II: *La Porte d'Enfer*

Eli appeared reluctant to cross over. Instead, we swung back to Hester Alley and the Naumkeag Harbor area. On the portico of a grand red brick building, he pointed to a replica of a half serpent half human that faced the water.

I assumed in jest, Eli signaled that I accompany him in the signs of the cross.

"The building is *La Porte d'Enfer*, and locals recite stories of having witnessed phantom armadas on the Atlantic's horizon that sail into shore to disgorge their cargo of shades. 'Emigres from Hades,' they profess."

III: The Holy Men

At that moment we saw walking toward us a trio of bearded men in black robes mumbling to themselves what I inferred was the liturgy of *The White Whale*.

"The Ishmaels," Eli explained. "MacLeish Sq.'s holy men. The carved whale-bone amulets about their necks are replicas of Queequeg's coffin."

"Is yours among them?" I asked.

He didn't reply.

IV: The Un-Christened Others

In their wake was an assemblage Eli referred to as "Others."

My immediate impression was one of sea birds barking in flight.

"They are a disquieted lot who manifest a chastened expression as if they are rightfully guilty for not having been chosen," Eli explained.

"They are the shades. The ill-starred ones who reside across the Charles in Netherland."

V: *Inferno* Passage

I dared not violate Eli's trust in me by manifesting any sign of disbelief, for I, too, was complicit in his narrative. I followed him as would a child through a magical wood.

Yet how could I not acknowledge that we had embarked on a downward passage? Why else would Eli have chosen the *Inferno* to escape the dark will to succumb?

The paralyzed tongue is no match for the voice that appears out of nowhere . . . and one that only its victim can hear. It has its own lexicon that was forged in Hell.

VI: Proctor's Sentience

The journey had now become our shared catechism.

Once Eli deigned to guide me through MacLeish Sq. and its fringes, he had no better idea than I where it might lead. For he was beholden to the voice that had taken residence in his psyche . . . and suffered a preternatural fear of surrendering to it.

I longed to tell Eli that the voice lingers immortal in the canopy of our souls.

VII: Crossing the Acheron

> There then he, Queequeg, sat holding the imbecile candle in the heart of that mighty forlornness. There then he sat, the sign and symbol of a man without faith, holding up hope amid despair.

Imagining the two of us aboard Charon's skiff, crossing the stygian Acheron, I envisioned myself in this very moment as the heathen harpooner in a cosmos Ishmael perceived as "a vast practical joke."

Was Eli, in the end, destined to be my life-buoy?

VIII: Queequeg's Candle

That evening I accompanied Eli to the tavern across from the Basilica. We stood several yards away in the shadows and watched as a woman attired all in black entered.

"The Falling Man Tavern," he said.

And is it any mystery that the only source of earthly light for the forlorn males had to be the wick of a woman's body?

Even in the scarce amber that bled from the streetlights through the square's foliage, I could see how emotional Eli had become.

Yes, why she, the Hester acolyte, had such a profound presence in and around Eli's MacLeish Sq.

Where the musk was embroidered red and she, the alley's namesake, came out mostly at dark, the winds off the harbor shadowed her and her male acolytes. Her singular presence more pronounced, dominant, than that of the numerous black-robed Ishmaels.

The latter carried no light under their black cloaks.

IX: Musk Embroidered in Red

Later that very same evening, Eli and I entered the hotel off the square, the one he'd designated Cotton Mather. We sat on one of the waiting room's chintz sofas.

Momentarily she appeared attired in her customary black, but now in place of the severe bun, her hair—glistening as if wet—fell freely on the collar of her coat. She wore black leather pumps that mirrored the corridor's amber lighting as she entered the *Souls of the Dead Dining Room*, the one bordered off by French doors.

X: Cotton Mather's Dance

Eli stood outside one of those doors peering in.

Of course, I knew what he was about to witness. During one of those nights in our bedroom he'd revealed exactly what to expect. And it was that illumined memory that militated against my very own. In truth I was viewing two experiences simultaneously, but mine paled in comparison.

She waited nearly motionless; her hands folded before her on the lace tablecloth.

It was at this moment Charon appeared and took his place at the piano. The gentleman at the head of the table, the one I recalled as Cotton Mather, stood and faced Charon.

"Please, Maestro, a melody for this wondrous occasion."

Whereas what I observed was Leah sitting alone at a table set for six in an empty dining room being served a glass of red wine by a lone waiter and listening to Stephen Tritos perform "Haunted Heart" on the Bosendorfer. But unlike earlier at the Falling Man, her right hand she now cradled in her lap and out of sight.

XI: A Self-Acquittal

Yet, like Eli, I too felt emotionally exhausted when we turned to head back to the Basilica, for the drama that continued to loop in my head was his.

"We exist in her shadow," I muttered.

Was not her indifference a means for her to remain untouched?

To salvage the vulnerability, she kept secreted inside her?

It's what, I believe, permitted her to walk about MacLeish Sq. with such a serene bearing. Or to sit in the same seat at the Falling Man, radiating a self-acquittal that was the envy of others.

XII: *So That I Will Forget You?*

Lying awake that night, I relived the evening when Eli had read a story of mine and perceived the strong association between its subject and Leah, my brother's lover.

On our final evening together, we knew it was unlikely we would meet again. When she put her coat on to leave, I asked her to stay.

"Why? So that I will forget you?"

It took me years to understand that only the memory of the

heady days and nights we'd spent together could endure . . . while our lives together in real life would not.

XIII: Pallor of the Dead

"From the pallor of the dead we borrow the expressive hue of the shroud in which we wrap them."

Perhaps that is what caught Eli as he gazed through my studio window. No one called or inquired, just as I had wished. For then I had to be somebody I no longer was.

Dead and loving it.

I gestured for him to come in. Now I was accompanying him through MacLeish Sq.

For all I knew it was somewhere in my past.

XIV: How Do We Bury Him?

The period I resided in the same house with Eli, always in the forefront of my mind was how each had sought after the other's approval.

Yet it was never enough.

Because that wasn't who I was.

"And the Eli you, John Proctor, presumed was me . . . was not," he would aver.

How do we bury him? I mused.

The paradox I found bitterly amusing.

Do we lay him to rest, or let those for whose approval he yearned do it?

Without knowing who might appear.

Their affirmations had grown cold.

XV: Nothing Is Real Here

Nothing is real here, I thought to myself.

"We're sleeping in a church whose raison d'être is as forlorn as are we. Even the rood installed above the choir loft glows neon red and jaundice yellow over those huddled beneath.

"It is as if we're trying to venerate what we are unworthy to recall."

Eli stood up and with his arms made a sweeping arc to all those gathered below in the nave and the choir loft; then he pointed to the side chapels.

"It's like they, including my Ishmael, are all grasping onto Quee-queg's casket.

"As if they are wary of themselves.

"The mortal fear that they had been abandoned?"

Eli slumped back onto the pew.

XVI: Odysseys Link Identities

"He no longer summons me home," he divulged. "*Do you know why?*

"I had no father except the one I made up in my head. The Ishmaels and their hallowed words comforted me.

"It was a most wonderful narrative I'd penned for myself.

"Until I wanted answers.

"But there are none in MacLeish Sq., are there?

"We, in truth, are those dead souls brought to the shores of Naumkeag by the ghostly armada. Willing to become who we never were. It is the acolytes of a former time who perpetuate the myth, that we were once loved by an entity larger than ourselves. 'Will we encounter Him in Naumkeag?' lingers on the lips of its settler shades."

Eli gathered up his belongings and motioned for me to follow. Prior to vacating the Basilica, he glanced over at Ishmael's side chapel.

"They commerce in death," he muttered.

"Thanatos cedes everlasting life to the believers."

Outside on the Basilica's steps and standing before *La Porte d'Enfer*'s bronze doors, Eli embraced me, whispering, "*There is no succor. Except the farce, that is.*"

He erupted in laughter.

"*In the belfry's theatre . . . paternity pales.*"

XVII: Manuscript's Nexus: Final Circle

"Do you see any illumination out in the water?" he asked.

But the still ocean only mirrored scant starlight.

"It's all gone, isn't it?" He motioned for us to sit down on the shoreline.

"What is it, Eli?"

"All of it. *Porte d'Enfer*, King Minos, Ghost Armada, Singing Trees, or a *Dining Room of the Dead Souls*. There is no Hester Alley or Falling Man Tavern. Drowned in the vortex of a boy's narrative. And MacLeish Sq.? Where is such a place as that, John Proctor? We can't return to it tonight, for it isn't there, is it? It has never been there."

"Yet it has been my home for as long as I can remember."

He turned to me, his face disfigured by anguish.

What is any one of us if cast out of our story? I thought.

"No, MacLeish Sq. exists, son. It's made my life richer and salvaged yours."

"Then what is the answer?"

"Like you discovered: there is none.

"Perhaps Ishmael is your authentic father, and for that we should be grateful. I couldn't have imagined him as you were able to, Eli. Every burg should have a Hester Alley. Every child a Queequeg lifebuoy amulet.

"*We only must take caution that we don't forfeit our authorship of the narratives themselves. By that I mean the imagined father summoning you had begun telling the story.*"

XVIII: Mendicants Who'd Crawled Back from Hell

"But what about the mendicants who didn't want to be identified with their ghosts?" he answered.

"Was it not the very same reason I had found my identity here? Had not the Melville tutor sanctified Eli?

"And what place better to exist within than stories that have already been written? The tales have already been consecrated. Those fortunate enough found redemption in the Basilica's side chapels and acceptance in the colloquies in and around Hawthorne's statue.

"Within months of receiving an Ishmael's nod of recognition, each moved about the square less reminisced.

"Like me, they were no longer themselves."

XIX: "What Took You So Long, Eli?"

Eli and I boarded a local bus that night, the first leg of our trip back home. He was especially depleted and kept falling off to sleep. It was as if he kept looking back, and upon waking would ponder the questions that continued to haunt him.

In one such instance, he awoke with a start.

"What was she teaching me, I'd ask myself while wandering about MacLeish Sq. in my felt suit, indifference?

"Was her ubiquitous black dress an analog of my Biely attire?

"Upon seeing me in it, might she find her countenance brighten because of what I have learned about life?

"*What took you so long, Eli?*'"

He broke into a wide grin before falling back into a deep sleep.

XX: Jeremiah's Burning: The Foreshadowing

We arrived at my house the following midnight.

Within minutes we were back in our bedroom. Prior to turning out his lamp, he muttered:

"Grateful to be home."

Yes, I thought. *For you have graced its rooms with your more luminous ones, a place to which only you could have ventured to visit and now have thankfully returned.*

I'm the richer for it. But that's too much for you to understand.

Within days, Eli and I had returned to our diurnal patterns and sharing meals together. He had begun writing in his journal and we had not yet resumed trading stories at bedtime.

Until the night he opened it and read the following:

As I feared, I saw my father. *Yes,* I thought, *there is no way you could be denied your insidious power over me.* I began weeping like I'd lost the battle and that the *Theatre of Toledo* had been nothing more than a farce to distract me from something that could never change. Who was I kidding? The Wood of Suicides was precisely that: people went there to call it quits. The self-inflicted violence to their bodies was no equal to what they suffered inside their heads.

In a moment of abject defeat, I lay back and waited. *Go on, say it,* I pled. *Let's get this over with.*

He stood there motionless, his countenance one of profound sadness, yet he said nothing. It was then I saw flames ripple up his body and travel out his arms, which, rising from his sides, began to flap as if they were wings.

Neither of us moved.

Just the two of us. One trying to escape, the other wanting to reach out and embrace . . . but was terrified of fire.

Eli switched off his bed lamp. And there in the Acheronian dark, inches above my body, levitated glowing Jeremiah. Grinning as if to say:

This is how you live forever, sweet brother.

The burning meadow concupiscence with Hestia accorded him life everlasting. Neither Eli nor I would ever outlive his visitations.

To think I once had felt anguish over Jeremiah's fearlessness.

CHAPTER TWELVE

ELI

For days following our return I found myself calling back this mental image:

It was then I saw flames ripple up his body and travel out his arms, which, rising from his sides, began to flap as if they were wings.

Neither of us moved.

Just the two of us. One trying to escape, the other wanting to reach out and embrace . . . but was terrified of fire.

Then, as if by design, while scouring John Proctor's bookshelves yet once again, I chanced upon a packet of manuscript drafts he had written years earlier, including the story "Celebrity." I'm certain he placed it there following my absence.

CELEBRITY

My brother gate-crashed Arlington National Cemetery. It was Jeremiah's penultimate prank. The three-rifle volley bugled "Taps," his casket draped by the American flag ceremoniously folded like an heirloom bedspread then handed off to his wife by a patent-leather-shod Marine. Even the tears. But there was no jumping out of the dirt cake this time, yelling, "Surprise!"

"Are you driving back with the undertaker?" she asked.

"I want to linger. I'll hitch a ride later," I said, watching the black cortege move formally toward Memorial Gate.

I tossed a pebble onto his embossed casket. "All right now,

Houdini, time to cut the shit and climb out of there. Everybody's gone home." The afternoon sun puddled his grave. If we had been kids and come upon the box in a meadow, we would have jerry-built cart wheels to its sides and fashioned a steering wheel at its prow. It was a handsome rig.

"Jeremiah, now don't be playing tricks on me. Why, Christ, you ain't even been in the military. (He'd been Sunday-soldiering in the Marine Reserves.)

"The grave tenders be here soon to pile a ton of dirt on your bloody ass. Now come on out!"

Jeremiah wasn't stirring.

"Shit, man—what's a joke if you ain't around to laugh about it?"

A clique of men in white coveralls crested the ridge and marched straight toward us, shovels resting like M-1 rifles on their right shoulders. With military precision they pitched the black earth into his hole. The first spadesful rained onto the copper roof in metronome time. If he was listening, he could hear it, too. Soon I no longer heard the pinging. Just soft earth raining upon itself—muffled like his voice.

"I warned you, didn't I? One day you'd take this business of shilling laughs too damn far. Who will ever give a shit that Jeremiah Daugherty slid his way under the gates of Arlington, singing, 'I got plenty of nothin', and nothin's plenty for me'?"

At the coda, the lead worker tossed the soil higher than usual. The earth retained the shape of a black spade—it floated in the half-light for a fugitive moment, then splattered on the ground.

"It may be Arlington to you, Brother, but it's marble city to them." Patching the wound with sod, the grave men tamped it down in a macabre line dance. As the formation marched back up the hill, I returned to the site. Jeremiah was down there deeper than one man could stand on another man's shoulders. Waves of sooty light rolled progressively across the ridge. I lay on the sod listening for a heartbeat but heard only cicadas from out beyond the spear-topped gate.

* * *

Lying down there was a sacrilege. Bad enough when Jeremiah set Josiah Cringle's hay field on fire. Burned a swatch right through it from the shoulder on Countyline road straight out into the middle where he collapsed—his pant legs burning like cattails soaked in benzene.

A charred scar down the center of the pasture.

Got called that Sunday afternoon to the hospital and met Jeremiah lying on a gurney in the emergency room, smoking. Mother fainted because she thought he was dead. His legs were swathed in gauze, as were his hands and arms. The orderly arced the cigarette to and away from his mouth mechanically.

My brother, as always, wearing a big shit-eatin' grin, "Now don't be alarmed, Ma. Ain't nothing more than a severe sunburn. Be out of here in a couple of days. Just lucky that old Ben here (he gestured to a dour stranger in a Marine uniform) saw me on fire, jumped out of his car 'n' rolled me into his overcoat and stamped the flame right out of my legs. Damnedest thing. I didn't feel a thing. Still don't, for that matter."

Ben muttered something to the effect that he had to stamp on Jeremiah to save him. Seems my brother's car had run out of gas, and he'd borrowed a can from a neighboring farmhouse, then carelessly poured some onto his clothes while priming Pap's carburetor. When he got the car going good again, he lit a cigarette. That's when the show opened.

"Sonofabitch, flames leapt like fire ants to my hands and arms. So, I got outta the car and began running through a field. The damn meadow was attacked by the ants, too. Christ, we were all burning."

"Why did you run, Jeremiah?" Pap asked.

"Don't know. Why'd I do it, Ben?"

The orderly gave Jeremiah another drag.

A week later we were again summoned to Harmony Memorial. In our dining room, a roll-away cot sat alongside the old Kimball upright awaiting his arrival. The mood was grim outside the ward's door. "Your son may not be coming home, Mr. Daugherty," the doctor said. "He's gone into shock. Third-degree burns. We're doing all we can to save him."

Instead of gladiolas, Jeremiah's body was surrounded by a mass of tubes and wires, causing him to look like he was a gauzed bird caught in a tangle of rural electric lines. Mother gripped the rail at the foot of his bed. His eyes were shut, but his face had a yellow cast to it that old stew chickens do.

Pap leaned down and whispered something in his ear.

Mother began keening. I stood over in the corner of the hospital room, trying to act grief-stricken like the others, but I knew something about Jeremiah none of them fully understood.

* * *

"You got to learn to treat death like a woman," he said one night as we lay in bed.

"What do you mean?"

"You can't be afraid of them, Westley."

"I ain't afraid of women."

"The real ones, you are," he said. "The kind that chew your balls off, huh? Not Jeremiah Daugherty. I grab their headlights and yank them right to me. Laugh in their cold faces. That's when they begin to bend. Well, let me tell you a secret, Brother . . . it's how you treat Mr. Taps, too. Blow smoke right back into his hairy face."

"How can you be sure?" I said.

"'Cause Mr. Taps smells like a woman. Do you think men hang themselves because they want to die? No, they do it because they smell cunt."

"You're full of shit, Jeremiah. Go to sleep."

"Listen to me. I'm trying to teach you something."

"How do you know?"

"I've smelled both. Ain't no difference."

"That death smells like a woman?"

"Under the armpits. Between the legs."

"You got a big imagination, too."

"Remember when you and me found Mama bent over the canning stove in the cellar with the Maytag cozy over her head?"

Headlights of passing cars flitted across our bedroom walls.

"And you carried her up the stairs into the living room crying for her to come alive—me, bawling like a ninny, running alongside, holding her hand like I wanted her to take me with her? And how you hollered for me to open the living room window so she could get air, then threw the damn glass figurine of some fairy through it . . . and the window crashed all over the living room floor like ice while you pumped on Mama's body?"

"Yes."

"Well, I ain't told you this, Westley, but when the stench of her dying began to fill the living room that Sunday afternoon—I knew. Death don't just creep through the walls. Maybe no footprints behind, maybe no notes, or pieces of raggedly clothing, but he does leave his perfume.

"Smells just like a woman. God's word."

I sat up in bed and stared at Jeremiah. His moon-lit face, like General Grant's on town common, was one of intense determination.

"You sure?" I said.

"Mama's alive, ain't she?"

"In the next room."

"Probably in Pap's arms. Same thing, Westley."

* * *

Arlington by now had succumbed to night. No moisture wicking up through the Toupée on my brother's grave.

"You got it all wrong, Jeremiah," I cried. "Wasn't Mr. Tap's fragrance you smelled. You just got a toxic whiff of Mama's lusting to die. She was in the heat of the act when we cut it short. Remember what she said when she came to? *'Why did you do that?'* Like she was scolding us, huh?

"But you, intoxicated by Mama's rutting, kept flying against her like a moth to a light bulb. Until Mama got her wish. *Except it's you, Jeremiah! Not her.*

"Out here among all these decorated stiffs. All eternity having to lie, pretending you were shot down over Cringle's farm. That your P-38 strafed the Union Trust Bank in downtown Harmony before it suddenly caught fire and you parachuted out of the sky, a torch.

Wearing all those bottle caps on your chest . . . you think these people won't be able to see through this?"

I began to roll the sod back off Jeremiah's grave.

"You're coming home with me! *'It was just a big goddamn foolish joke of my brother's, sir.' That's what I'll say. 'Please excuse us. I'll just put a dolly under this oversized fancy copper box here and wheel him back to Harmony where the fuck he belongs.'*

"Hold on, brother. I'll be there soon."

But the digging was tedious. A fog had crept over the burial grounds, veiling a gibbous moon. I had to feel the edges of the great lawn's lesion.

"Don't let your ass get too comfortable now."

I dug throughout the night, striking copper by dawn. At the first sign of sun slowly rising over Arlington's crest, it flooded onto Jeremiah's casket like fire. Just as I had imagined—as I had worked above him through the night, he had labored below me.

The catafalque didn't have spoked cart wheels . . . instead, Jeremiah had stretched a kind of parchment, or goatskin, over a skeleton of wings—a Fokker—and added a tail to its rear. They were fragile appendages. Sunlit gossamer, locusts' wings almost, about to flap this coffin out of Arlington.

"No, Jeremiah, I don't smell a goddamn thing! I swear." To the nose of the bier I attached a propeller . . . not of a common sort, but fabricated out of two shovels, yoked end to end. Two giant spoons. Their black blades ready to scoop the air into a wind that would lift us heavenward.

"Jeremiah, we're going to do it!"

And I climbed out of the grave. The box lay glinting in the sun. Its parchment wings and tail, translucent.

"Hurry," I cried. "Before the Squad returns."

Like a locust, the bier's wings began to pulsate. The fuselage of humanity lifting, levitating the copper box out of Arlington's hole.

"Jeremiah! Where are you?"

The box hovered inches above the earth's massive wound, the sun Blakian on its body, its locust-chattering deafening. Slowly the lid began to open to the morning, the scent of gladiolas and roses wafting out of its interior.

"Climb in," he calmly said. "We're going home."

I peered into the hovering contraption. He lay there, smirking, as I would have been disappointed if he hadn't. Outfitted in Marine dress, sporting a shiny visored officer's cap. He had gold stripes on his coat sleeves and a legion of combat ribbons on his breast. But the satin blanket still covered his legs.

"Come on, dammit. We can't hover indefinitely," he barked.

I climbed in and the contraption began to lift off. Up over the crest of the hill. Then we started to go down the other side. "Slow down!" I cried.

But Jeremiah was having none of it.

"Jesus Christ, Jeremiah, we're going too fast!"

A gleam in his eye like the day I saw him following the scarring of Cringle's grassland. About to yank her headlights to him. Like he was going to fuck her. I put my feet out of the bottom of the contraption's fuselage, skidding the macadam.

"God almighty, Jeremiah, we're going to crash!"

Jeremiah was now laughing, yanking on one side of the cart's wheels with Mother's clothesline, then tugging on the other. The spoked wheels we'd purloined off a neighbor's baby buggy were twisting, wobbling like they'd lost their strength, too. Now both my feet were dragging on the tar, smoking the leather right off them.

I shoved my head into Jeremiah's lap, holding onto him for dear life, the *Death-smells-like-a-woman pilot*, and squeezed hard. But Jesus be my witness, squeezed air—for there was no Jeremiah. All dress uniform. Weren't a soul inside. Just medals, stripes, and golden epaulets.

The fuselage on the contraption's wings and tail his own. Glinting in the sun like bird skin over bone. Blue veins its tracery. A bag of bile its heart.

When the soapbox went headlong through the plate glass window, Jeremiah yelled:

"Do you smell her yet, Westley? *Now are you afraid?*"

While reading, I felt as if I were violating what I wasn't supposed to know. *Why else would the man who kept summoning me home appear before me on fire?*

But I chose not to talk about it.

* * *

John Proctor and I had settled into each passing day's rhythm. I was unsure if I was responding so favorably to his happiness or my escape from MacLeish Sq . . . a home that wasn't always so.

One evening he led me into his studio, wanting to show me a canvas he had been working on.

He believed he'd broken through a shell of his own making. "Perhaps I thought I was safe inside it, Eli. But all that has occurred since, including our sojourn in Naumkeag, has introduced me to a former self."

He began chuckling and gestured as if that "stranger" was standing next to us.

"Those nights across from each other in our bedroom, you'd read stories of mine that I swear on my beloved brother's grave, *The poor soul who penned those laments has up and gone because I, John Proctor, sure as hell didn't write them.*

"And then it hit me: I wasn't aware that he *had* abandoned me. Just the husk of his person resides in those dust-gathering journals. Like he laid down his life in words . . . then vanished."

John Proctor strode to his easel and lifted a cloth veiling the painting.

It was a fragmentary sketch of a man on fire, hovering in the air, his arms extended like wings in flight.

Blazing carmine, blue, and orange shades.

The body and face of the individual suggested by a feathery image.

He and I locked eyes.

"Familiar?" he asked.

Yes, it's your deceased brother, Jeremiah, I thought but said nothing.

"I couldn't fall asleep after you had described what you witnessed, Eli. *He* appeared before me, too. Alive, like I could reach out and touch him."

We stood there, searching each other's expression.

Until he broke eye contact and drew the cloth back over the canvas.

"Will you be joining me for lunch today?"

I begged off, saying I'd planned to walk to town.

John Proctor caught me at the door. "Eli, I've a surprise for you."

He pointed to the studio window, the very one years earlier I'd peered through.

"I think it's time you learned how to drive.

"Out there in the driveway is a car. Been in storage for several years."

That afternoon he sat alongside as I drove the aged Plymouth ragtop down our backwoods' gravel roads, the windows open wide and radio blasting country music. It was of a stick-shift and clutch vintage. We joyed at my lurching us forward, and when I finally got the hang of it, he sat back and pulled a pack of cigarettes out of the glove compartment.

"My secret sin," he grinned, signaling I join him.

Before long we were singing along with tunes on the radio while filling the interior of the car with velvety blue smoke.

* * *

Upon returning home that evening, he handed me the Plymouth's key.

"The ragtop's yours, Eli. I'll help you get ready to take the driver's test. Then you're free, my friend. Take it anywhere your heart desires. It even has a rumble seat."

Speechless, I stood there staring at him.

"We'll keep the smokes in the glove compartment, okay?"

Each of us broke out laughing, at which point John Proctor placed his arms around me, muttering, "Welcome home, Son."

As I look back upon that day, what strikes me most is the gift of that cream two-seater convertible and how for real it was. That night in bed I could see it from the window. It existed outside my consciousness in a way that nothing ever had in that same way. I didn't have to imagine it. The ragtop sat there waiting for me to drive it off at will. It was as if the gentleman had given me the ultimate gift . . . something truly alive outside my head.

A place where I'd resided for perhaps too long.

He instinctively understood that. *Welcome home, Son. Here's the key.*

I'd never felt alive in this way.

The next morning at daybreak, I was outside cleaning and polishing the beauty, which even sported white sidewalls. Its odometer read thirty-two thousand miles, and I figured the car had been back and forth across the States several times. Immediately I began daydreaming of where I'd take it and what music stations I'd find on the illuminated red dial.

The stick shift even had been appointed with an alabaster cue ball handle.

John told me that shortly after he moved back to his hometown, he spotted the Plymouth in a gas station with a "for sale" sign on its windshield.

"Like you, Eli, I fell in love with it on the spot. It had belonged to the owner's son who had joined the service. I believe I gave him four hundred dollars for it and drove it here with the top down, feeling like an aged-cat's ass. At best I've probably put less than a couple thousand miles on it since. So, it's been sitting in a rented garage piling on the years . . . like me.

"Lucky for both of us, you came along."

As the days and weeks passed, MacLeish Sq. began to recede ever further into the past. There were times I became conflicted about that truth, questioning how one world that was all I knew had dissolved into another as foreign to me at first. But then it would pass.

I had more important things to concern myself with, like parallel parking with an officer of the law sitting alongside.

One day when we were on a practice run out on one of the country lanes, and I was passing a car in front of us, he noticeably stiffened. Once I made the maneuver, I asked, "Did I do something wrong?"

"Not really," he said. "You just remind me of my brother."

I slowed down.

"Jeremiah would chide me for being afraid to take risks. *'And your reward is what . . . an extra helping of years? Why, if you can't taste 'em, Bro?'"*

He pulled the smokes from the glove compartment while switching on the radio.

"Describe him for me?"

"Very little bothered the kid, even at a young age. My being three years his senior meant nothing to him. In truth, I vicariously lived through his audaciousness. Having bought the whole package of Mother's church teachings, including that Jesus was my conscience, I dared not disappoint her or Christ. Jeremiah thought that was funny as hell. She had tacked an acidic-green glow-in-the-dark Crucifix above the bed we shared as boys. He'd delight in sliding it down my briefs, illuminating my genitals.

"'That's your conscience, Johnny,' he'd jibe."

Each of us was smoking now, and he'd found a station playing Stan Kenton recordings.

"You were considered the *good* brother?"

"I guess, but the kid always took the applause . . . even from her. For years we'd lie awake on a Saturday night in the wee hours waiting for our father to tumble blind drunk out of one of his cronies' cars, then crawl to our kitchen door in the back yard. She'd be there to greet him and that's when all hell would erupt. Jeremiah would stand at the top of the stairs and give me a radio announcer's static blow-by-blow on the downstairs' mayhem. I didn't want to hear. Come Sunday, she took to her bed with the window blinds drawn. Like someone had perished.

"Her worst fear was that her sons would become just like the old man and she direly threatened either of us if we ever touched the stuff. Well, shy of his fifteenth birthday, Jeremiah attended a friend's wedding and returned home after midnight shitfaced, staggering to the kitchen door. But instead of entering, he climbed onto the picnic table in our back yard and commenced warbling, "My Melancholy Baby" up to Mother's bedroom window.

"Envisioning her in a fiery rage of grief and anger, I feared that she was going to take her own life—since she had threatened as much for years—but first would take my brother's too. I leapt out of bed and ran into the hall to stop her. Except the door to their bedroom never opened. Father hadn't returned home yet.

"Before long, the kid stumbled up the stairs and crawled into bed with his clothes on.

"The next morning, I arose early and was surprised to see her setting the table for breakfast. Neither of us said a word about what had transpired the night before. An hour passed before she called up the stairwell: 'Jeremiah, what would you like for breakfast?'

"'Pancakes!' he cried."

The expression on John Proctor's face was one of stark bewilderment.

"Jesus, Eli. The little prick melted her melancholy heart."

When I pulled into a roadside tavern, he was still caught up in the moment.

"Was there anything Jeremiah was afraid of?"

"Yes. *Felo-de-se.*"

* * *

When we sat down and ordered drinks, it became apparent he didn't want to continue the conversation.

But that evening before we turned out our bedroom lamps, he asked if he could read me something.

"This may help explain how I answered your question earlier today, Eli."

Jeremiah Only Laughs Come Twilight

I often envision Jeremiah at twilight waving to me from a neighbor's window or a passing automobile.

I've no idea what is going on in his mind, but for me it's a host of memories and emotions tumbling forward.

Mostly I long for him to utter my name. It's really all I wish. I cry, "Ethan. I'm Ethan. Read my lips." He breaks out in laughter as if it were some diabolical joke we share.

There are enough of them.

For it was he who ran down to the ballpark where I was working the concession stand, a night game, bawling that he'd found Mother slumped over a gas stove in our basement.

Does that memory bubble up in his consciousness? It does mine when we wave to each other.

Or how about the night we were home alone and Mrs. Izzo, our neighbor, knocked on our kitchen window, motioning for us to hurry outside. She was as white as the sheets and pillowcases she laundered and dried on her clotheslines for a living. "Your momma's up the street. You better go up there and find her."

Well, up our street was a limestone quarry, a rendezvous for the sick at heart who leaped to their watery deaths. "How do you know?" I asked. "You're too young to understand," she said. Our street was notorious for the quarry's fatal attraction. Seldom would a year go by where it wasn't mentioned more than once in the obituary page. There were occasions long after midnight that Jeremiah and I would be on our knees gazing out the window at somebody walking up the street alone. Soon they'd disappear beyond where the streetlights stopped, and we knew they'd never walk back down.

That night Jeremiah ran ahead of me, each of us terrified of what we might find. "Momma, Momma," he cried—hoping she'd step out from between one of the houses. But when there were no more houses and we were enveloped in total darkness, I joined in. Our calls echoing each other. A glade of hemlock and white birch surrounded the quarry like a monk's tonsure. Once inside it, Jeremiah turned to me, stricken. "She's floating in that water down there, ain't she,

Ethan? Bodies rise to the surface like soap in the bathtub, don't they? Tell me, Ethan, you know she's down there. Ain't she?"

I didn't want him to see. Jeremiah had such a wild imagination that he could make me laugh. But he could also make me cry. I told him to wait, and I would look. "How will you be able to see her, 'cause it's dark? No moon shining into the quarry's bowl." Except I knew how she'd prepared for the gas burner incident.

"She'll be white in her petticoat . . . just like the soap bar," I replied.

I left Jeremiah and was about to peer over the quarry's ledge, when I heard my name called. I turned and she was standing there barefoot in her rayon slip.

Peaceful-like, alongside a tangle of white birch trees. Like her demons had all vanished.

"Momma?"

"What are you doing here, Ethan?"

Strange . . . as if I'd come to do what she was planning to do.

I stared at her.

It was almost as if we were strangers.

"I've come to take you back home, Momma. Jeremiah and me."

"Oh," she said, gazing down at her body.

"Well, I can't go like this. Can I? What will the neighbors think?"

"Mrs. Izzo said we'd find you here, Momma."

I gingerly approached and held out my hand to her. "Come, Momma. It's getting late. Jeremiah and me have to get to bed for school tomorrow."

As if in a dream she came to me, and we began walking back through the woods toward Jeremiah.

When he spotted the two of us, he began sobbing, thinking that it was her ghost. For in the darkness her moonlit ashen slip rustled as she walked.

"Momma's comin' home with us, Jeremiah." As the three of us wandered out of the woods, he and I were unsure of who was walking between us. Weren't certain who she was except being our mother. And just before we reached the street, she stopped, pointing to a grocery sack containing clothes she'd secreted by a hemlock tree.

"Let me get presentable, boys. I don't want Mrs. Izzo or any of the other old women on the street to be talking about us."

It was one o'clock that morning when we stepped back into our house. Everything had clicked back into focus once again. Momma had returned to herself.

"I'll pack your school lunches in the morning," she said. "Now hurry on to bed."

* * *

When I catch Jeremiah waving to me and grinning from behind the glass on yet another evening, I question if he's off to where Momma used to go. Is he wandering about the lip of the quarry like she did? Has he been severed from all the terrible things that went through our minds on such occasions, so they no longer haunt him as they still do me?

If so, I'm happy for him.

But why can't he just once utter my name?

So, I'll know that when we pass through the glade of hemlock and white birch to peer over the quarry's lip and discover a soap bar in a petticoat floating to the surface of Lethe . . . we'll find a way to explain it to ourselves somehow.

Because I can't.

And Jeremiah only laughs come twilight.

"It's a piece I wrote when you went away. Maybe if he hadn't been so young, I reckon Momma's dark side wouldn't have mattered to him. Same as hardly anything did.

"Especially when he reached his teens.

"Until the night I told him I was leaving home for good.

"From the start he and I had shared the same bed. It was a month or two following my eighteenth birthday and time for me to say goodbye. I'd bought a used car with my savings from work and was determined to strike out on my own.

"Jeremiah mutely watched my every move that night as I packed up. He trailed me to the car, and we still hadn't exchanged a word or engaged in eye contact.

"When it was time to go, I pulled him close. 'Jeremiah . . .'

"He looked up at me, sobbing.

"Like he'd sworn never to do it again after that first incident with our mother. There had been others. Perhaps it had been his braggadocio on my behalf . . . or his.

"'What is it, brother? This is so unlike you,' I said. "Christ, how can we ever forget each other?'

"'You can't leave me here alone, Ethan.'

"Then I understood.

"Momma was watching us from the kitchen window."

* * *

That night I was unable to fall asleep for several hours. Why had Jeremiah surfaced so prominently in John Proctor's preconscious? I thought about his and my relationship since returning from MacLeish Sq. That vintage car he'd gifted me. Had he kept it stored in some garage in his brother's memory? Then I came along.

It had begun to feel as if Jeremiah were living in the next room. Perhaps I was wearing his clothes. Had the key to his car. I sat up in bed and glanced over at John. He had been watching me.

"What is it, Eli?"

"When I was a boy, there was this place she longed to go. I'd dance for her, and she'd say, 'Where are we going, Eli?' And I'd answer, 'Toledo.'

"That was Jeremiah's ghost, too, wasn't it?"

"Yes.

"'*She'll be white in her petticoat . . . just like the soap bar.*' The image of her floating in our quarry blossomed in his young mind.

"It clung to him like a nettle."

* * *

The next morning when we sat down together at the breakfast table, he smiled and said, "Eli, there's a poem by Fernando Pessoa I wish to share with you.

Nothing of nothing remains. We're nothing.
In the sun and air we put off briefly
The unbreathable darkness of damp earth
Whose weight we'll have to bear—
Postponed corpses that procreate.
Laws passed, statues seen, odes finished—
All have their grave. If we, heaps of flesh
Made sanguine by an inner sun,
Must set, then why not they?
We're tales telling tales, nothing . . . [xxii]

"That's what last evening was about: *We're tales telling tales, nothing . . .*"

He gestured to the ragtop outside the kitchen window.

"Knowing you as well as I believe I do by now, I suspect it has occurred to you that it might have once belonged to Jeremiah."

I didn't reply.

"Well, it didn't. But it is a close replica of the one that sat outside our bedroom window in a gravel driveway. It's why he lived to awaken each morning, so he could climb into it. Even just to sit there and think about all the places he would go. That fucking motor car. She's what he wanted to be wedded to.

"Glinting in the morning sun instead of a dream that kept him awake and wouldn't let him go. In our bed at night Jeremiah would ask me to name him a state, 'Any state,' he'd say. I'd pick one out and he'd rattle off the capital, population, the sites inside it he planned to drive to, and then he'd sit up in bed mimicking how the people living there spoke. Christ, he'd have me near pissing our bed. And do you know why he was so funny, Eli?

"*'Cause Momma, floating like a gardenia in our quarry, wasn't.*

"Even the bar of soap in our bathtub had the perfume of death. His racing across the forty-eight, double-shifting over the asphalt ribbons of this land, recalling all the fucking stupid statistics just so he could keep his mind occupied . . .

"But, Christ knows, Eli, my brother couldn't race fast enough.

"That's why, Son, don't linger on the stuff that we passaged through last night.

"It's *the unbreathable darkness of damp earth* that will draw us down."

* * *

John Proctor gazed at me *"with a crucifixion in his face."*

As if he, Ishmael, was sitting up in the bed across from me. That he had evanesced out of Melville's tale to tell his own.

And that in some way I had become Jeremiah because he wanted the story rewound. Why else was I in this place, at this time? What was Ishmael's catechism that I took to heart in MacLeish Sq.? Was I being groomed for this moment, this occasion?

Who was my father? Ishmael? John Proctor?

How could I escape believing that the story I found myself in wasn't mine?

That clotted-cream ragtop outside the bedroom window, was it, so to speak, a replica of Queequeg's casket? Had Jeremiah fitted it out to travel across the states?

> *iron part of harpoon and one paddle, biscuits lined the sides, flask of fresh water at head, small bag of woody earth at the foot and a piece of sail cloth rolled up for a pillow.*[xxiii]

No grotesque figures adorning the coupe, save the pearly white cue ball festooning its stick shift and rabbit's foot dangling from its windshield mirror. Pint of Seagram's in the glove compartment and a radio whose dial glows red come dark when there's nothing to see.

Was it destined to become my life-buoy?

And hanging from the ragtop's rear bumper, thirty ropes ending in large knots for grasping.

CHAPTER THIRTEEN

JOHN PROCTOR

"The unbreathable darkness of damp earth . . ."

We'd head out for day trips.

It didn't matter where we'd go. Eli would take the wheel of the ragtop. He'd christened it *Mercy*.

"Oh, Mercy," he'd laugh, "where will you deliver two sinners today?"

One morning he headed to an amusement park in a nearby state. Eli had never been to one before. It was the Wildcat, a roller coaster, that he couldn't get enough of. I joined him twice, but then he went solo thrice again.

Alongside him then from a distance, I was witnessing the young man's birth from out of the mother ghost that had haunted him all his early years.

On Eli's final run, he stepped out of the car, dripping perspiration.

"Oh, John, why wasn't there a roller coaster in Naumkeag?"

"Puritans . . . too much fun."

"May Christ have mercy on their souls," he piously intoned, before hurrying off to the fun house whose sole entrance was a rotating oaken barrel the height of two men through. One had to navigate it to get to the room of mirrors. After being toppled several times and spit out the other side, I stood and watched Eli try.

Except he succumbed to the barrel sweeping him up one side

then letting him drop back down as though lifeless. He had no intention of ever getting out.

Others waiting to run through soon became impatient and started to yell at him.

Embarrassed, I jumped back into the barrel and grabbed his arm. We were ejected by centrifugal force.

Eli thought it was a hoot.

And once in the room of a dozen life-size mirrors, each reflecting yet another distorted version of oneself, he stood miming before each.

Until he came to the final one stationed at the entrance for the room with rotating walls and a floor that jostled up, down, and sideways.

In that mirror Eli saw his undistorted self.

Disquietingly, he stared back at his image, the joy whistling out of him.

Back out on the midway, I led him over to the concession stand. "Cheer up," I admonished him. "There's still the tunnel of love."

That was how many of our excursions went. There always seemed to be an instance when a setback occurred, and he was sucked into the vortex of his past. I could usually humor him out of it.

Later that day, we shared a seat on a small wooden boat that floated in a trough open to the elements for several yards before entering an ink-black tunnel. Only the purling water beneath us evidenced we were being ferried forward.

I couldn't help but question what was projecting inside Eli's head. Charon? The River Styx?

When, suddenly aborting this interminable period of total darkness, a woman in a red kerchief appeared to float before us, attended by the strains of Eric Satie's "*Gymnopédie* No. 1." Attired in a black coat with fur trimming, she glanced at us through a window with multiple panes.

Just as were about to surrender to the trance, we exited the tunnel and were drawn up a tracked incline. The clatter of the cogs catching into the iron tracks beneath us was deafening as we struggled to adjust to the intense sunlight. At the very top of the several-story steep incline, our small craft teetered, threatening to plummet us backwards into the tenebrous tunnel.

Eli didn't dare stand. The dory hung suspended for several moments before shooting us bow first into the drink, soaking us both to the skin.

"Mercy!" Eli jibed.

That night before we turned off our bed lamps, Eli pondered the identity of the woman in the red kerchief. "Her presence was so damned alien in that murky crypt," he said. "I'd have expected a clown or a hideous ghoul to jump out at us. But she came out of a dream."

"I've seen her before," I said.

"You have?"

"In one of my art books."

"Christ, who but you, Proctor, would embellish a fifteen-cent amusement park ride!"

"Which she sublimely erased for several moments, didn't she?"

"Beckoning us where, John?"

The noteworthy silence in our room lingered until broken by the exhaust of a passing car outside the house.

* * *

The following morning, when I passed Eli's room, I saw resting on his shelf an open book displaying *The Red Kerchief* by Claude Monet. After several outings I began to perceive a pattern. Those that especially struck him in some manner, he'd collect as a memento of our trip and display it among the others in his room as reminders that what he'd experienced had been real, tangible, not an experience he'd imagined.

I recall one such event that occurred during our first winter back from MacLeish Sq. There was a farm pond a couple of miles from our house. When it froze solid, the family who owned it would string lights and open it for paid skating. A shack had been erected at its edge, and inside, benches aproned a large cast-iron wood stove. A loudspeaker blared popular songs throughout the evening.

Eli had never ice skated before. I'd bought him a pair of skates one afternoon, surprising him at suppertime. Once it grew dark, we headed to the pond. I'd been there numerous times as a teen and still owned my pair. Virtually nothing had changed about the place except the music wafting over the pond.

The first couple times we tentatively circled the ice together, I assisted keeping him from falling. Soon he was navigating the mirror-like pond in wide arcs, lost in a reverie.

I returned to the enclosure for warmth, and it was at least another hour before I saw Eli again, entering with a young woman. They were giggling and conversing like old friends. He acknowledged my presence with a brief glance as the pair took a seat next to the stove, its cast iron radiating a fiery-orange glow.

Curiously, the young lady struck me as similar, though a more youthful version, to the woman in *The Red Kerchief*. Her black woolen outer coat was trimmed in white rabbit fur with Chinese frog closures and a Goya-red knit scarf veiling her ringleted raven hair. After spending several minutes rubbing their hands above the stove, they departed.

I watched from the lone window in the shed. The couple commenced skating in wide arcs, their legs moving in tandem and time as one.

Near closing time, only Eli, his new friend, and two other couples remained on the ice. I was standing at the doorway trying to get his attention when at the downbeat of a jump tune, Eli grabbed the young woman's kerchief, and with her clutching its other end, he began to pull her in a wide circle over the pond. At its outermost edges there were still soft areas marked by hand-lettered signs citing danger. He teased several of these as they flew about its periphery. She was laughing and Eli wore an expression I'd only seen when he was gassing Mercy down some country lane . . . It chided me not to worry.

If enabled, he would have gathered her off her feet and skated over the snow-covered meadows surrounding the ice.

Had he ever been this close to a girl?

That evening only the drone of Mercy's heater accompanied

our ride home. When he stepped out of the car, I handed him the red knit glove that had fallen out of his jacket, knowing then it was just a matter of time until he and I would no longer share the same bedroom.

Under similar circumstances, it had happened with Jeremiah.

"Her name's Alma," Eli said when we turned out the lights.

She was all he could talk about in the coming days. They went skating several more times without me. One Saturday night he took her to a movie and brought her home, where they spent most of that evening in his room. From downstairs I could hear him doing most of the talking and then realized he was reading Alma stories. Were they his or mine? As it was getting late, I became worried about her getting home before midnight.

They were sitting on the floor . . . she in one corner and he in the other, with his journals lying about him. Eli never looked up when I entered.

"Alma," I said, "they must be getting concerned about you at home. Eli, perhaps you'd better drive her back before it gets any later."

"Oh?" he replied, staring at her.

By then she was standing alongside me at the door with her coat on as if I had come to rescue her.

A few phone exchanges transpired between them in the week following. But Eli ceased mentioning her.

He had begun spending time again in his bedroom. And Mercy sat idle in the driveway.

"What's happened?" I asked one morning at breakfast.

"About what?"

"That lovely young lady with the raven curls and laughing face?"

"She's still around."

"What died?"

"Nothing *died*."

"From my window, Eli."

Eyes averted, he shot back, "She had no stories."

In my mind's eye I was still witnessing him draw her in sweeping arcs over the ice that first evening . . . Alma being whipped from one side to the other while clutching the end of her red kerchief, Eli driving backwards.

"Do you understand?"

I shook my head.

"That night in my room I read to her, hoping to provoke something she had imagined and felt inspired to share. A memory of her yearning, say, or silly happiness . . . it didn't matter to me.

"But I could only make her laugh on ice.

"We had nothing in common. I mistook her silence as an expression of interest."

"Did you tell her about MacLeish Sq.?"

He nodded.

"I'm certain she does have stories, Eli. They just aren't like yours."

* * *

Several days later, with my encouragement, he announced he was going to survey the "Wonders of the 48" with Mercy, and that he'd dispatch by mail to me a token that was emblematic of each stop. When I'd gifted Eli the car, I also set up a bank account in his name so that he wouldn't feel totally dependent on me.

A week passed and I received the first: a postcard with no writing other than my address but a photo of the courthouse in Ames, Iowa.

Then the tokens arrived regularly in two- or three-day intervals. A Polaroid of Eli sitting in a forest-green rowboat moored on the Upper Peninsula, Michigan lakeside grass; a words-only decal of the Golden Gate Bridge; a chiaroscuro postcard of the Hoover Dam with a replica of Mercy cut from a magazine pasted on its reverse side.

Then nothing. Each time the telephone rang, I ran to lift its receiver. Eli was never on the other end.

At week three, his mailings commenced once again. Except now each envelope contained a photo-booth sepia of Eli staring expressionless into the camera. I had to believe he was searching out penny arcades and fairgrounds in various cities and states so he could record another photograph of himself of having traveled there. No handwritten message ever, save the postmark on the envelope. Of the seven nondescript photos, in only one Eli was attired in a white Stetson and a pearly-buttoned cowboy shirt.

Exactly what he wore when he stepped out of Mercy at the close of his two-month odyssey.

Over dinner and drinks that night, Eli regaled me with reading from his travel journal a story, while mentioning that he had floated in the Great Salt Lake like a white bar of soap.

Blue Phantom and Saltair, Utah

I couldn't picture myself walking on water like Jesus.

Like any other adventure, some pieces of truthful information would get embellished by ample make-believe, so by the time I arrived—I'd be in for a big letdown.

The rain had begun to pour down. It must have been close to midnight when I saw flashing lights up ahead.

My eyeglasses were missing one lens. I'd carelessly dropped them in a gas station shortly after my departure. My driver's license stated that I had to wear corrective lenses while operating a vehicle. I could see well through only one eye.

"Good evening, officer. What's the trouble?"

The policeman shined his flashlight into my face.

"Where you headed?"

"Salt Lake City."

"Keep an eye out for the Blue Phantom," he warned. "Blew open the head of a lady from Georgia just up ahead of you a half hour ago."

"What's the Blue Phantom?"

He talked like I was supposed to know.

"He's blowing out windshields?"

Just then I passed a blue Willys Sedan that had veered off the road into a field of corn. Several police cars surrounded it, all their lights blinking. You could see its windshield had been shattered.

I scrunched down in my seat. If you'd been standing outside Mercy, you couldn't have seen my head. I could barely see over the hood.

I imagined the Blue Phantom might be perched in one of the towering country elms we rolled under.

When I pulled safely into a 76 truck stop at dawn, I asked a waitress if she knew who the Blue Phantom was.

"You one of his friends?"

"Seems he blew a hole through a lady's head on the highway back there," I said.

"Ain't nobody knows who he is," she said. "But he's a killer, that's for damn sure. I probably served him pancakes 'n' sausage this very morning. He comes out like the deathwatch beetle. Blows some stranger's head off through a windshield, then the police get all buzzed up. Blue goes underground again. May be my boss, for all I know."

"Why do they call him the Blue Phantom?"

She licked the lead on her pencil and added up our bill on her pad, slipping the check under my cup of coffee. "Where you from?"

"Harmony, Pennsylvania," I offered.

"Oh, yeah? Well, you can figure out for yourself the 'phantom' part."

"I was keeping my eyes peeled for a blue Chevy or something," I said.

"Ain't got nothing to do with the color."

"No?"

"No. This poor sonofabitch is blue, honey. The bluest psycho in all the Midwest. Ain't enough country and western songs on the juke machines in every damn truck stop from here to Reno to match how blue this poor sonofabitch is feeling. Bluer than all those moon-howlers locked in the county sanitorium you drove by coming through here.

"Harmony, Pennsylvania, huh?"

I took off my one-eyed glasses. "You say you were spotting for a blue Chevrolet?" she guffawed, touching my hand. "That's rich."

It began to dawn on me, after recalling the Blue Phantom experience, that the real world was indeed a mixture of truth and lies. That some men, like the Phantom, were trying to jump off.

It wasn't too many miles before I could see the sun dip like a yolk over the rim of a mighty calm plate of azure blue water. Until I saw the Atlantic, I thought Lake Erie was the ocean—its steel-blue roily waters, waves sometimes as high as town hall. On the opposite side of the Utah highway, a refinery spewed a foul sulfuric fog over the terrain.

I pulled Mercy off the road in toward the lake—no boats or sails on its horizon—and stripped to my underwear. *How far did I have to walk until I popped up?* The lake tasted exactly like Adam's ale with a salt chaser. Soon I was unable to touch bottom . . . but splashing to keep from bobbing onto my face. Eventually I sat in the drink as if I'd an inner tube about my stomach. A white-boy-from-the-East lily pad floating in the Great Salt Lake basin.

Could I walk on water? I couldn't, but I'd never have to worry about drowning again either. It was miraculous. As twilight turned into evening, I drifted about in the lake, the shoreline now a continent away . . . wafting in a watery half-light toward Nevada.

I saw spotlights washing the night sky and castle turrets illuminated with hundreds of flickering bulbs.

"*Saltair,*" I thought, and paddled to shore. In Mercy's headlights I looked porcelain. It was very difficult to see the road, even worse than when I had driven from Harmony.

As I wheeled down a gravel trail—the amusement park looked like it was floating on a colossal barge at the Great Salt Lake's periphery—a glaring spotlight materialized. I presumed I was merely moving closer to it than it to me. *It must be the entrance to Saltair*, I decided, and didn't slow down.

I hadn't seen Alma in a month. Just to get a whiff of a woman's perfume or smell her hair . . .

When this miniature star looms comet-bright a car's length away. I slammed on the brakes. A grinding noise of metal screeching against metal, tons and tons of it. Mercy and I are catapulted back off the roadway a good ten feet into the salt flats. The light that had been gradually blinding me now sat ocular at my windshield.

"Oh, my God!" voices screamed.

A giraffe pointed at Mercy's radiator.

"Mister, your water's burst!" It gestured a leg to liquid rivulating out from under the chassis. I climbed out of the car. Behind the giraffe and hanging over the locomotive's cowcatcher were a bulb-nosed clown dressed in blue, one mouse, and two Bo Peeps—all chorusing, "OH, JESUS!"

The giraffe signaled to the engineer, "He's okay, Tom!" Hissing steam shot out of the iron horse's belly. Mercy's headlights looked puny in the carnival train's glow. I apologized to the assemblage and stood in shock while the clown commiserated with his passengers. The front bumper was now shaped in a V-for-Victory. Worst of all, unsalted water hemorrhaged rust out of a gash in the radiator.

I turned the engine over. Thank God it began idling. The mouse and giraffe waved from the caboose until swallowed by night.

I prayed the water would hold before the temperature gauge began to panic and I could find a mechanic. But I felt as outcast and confused as surely the Blue Phantom had. I thought about the taller-than-men animals, the illuminated clown and Bo Peeps circling the Great Salt Lake where, like Jesus, nobody would ever drown unless they willed it.

I, of course, had written the story decades earlier and asked Eli if he'd purchased the cowboy hat and pearly buttoned shirt in Toledo. He laughed—first time—and shook his head.

"No. Cheyenne, Wyoming."

* * *

At daybreak I surveyed the damage to Mercy. It was apparent that Eli had stopped at junkyards along the way to replace the Plymouth's 1936-cylinder chromium radiator cover. Its front bumper was restored to its original shape and appearance except for a vertical weld at its center that resembled an appendectomy scar.

Otherwise, the automobile appeared shined and spotless as before his journey.

We continued to share breakfast together, yet lunch was out. There even were instances when I couldn't coax him downstairs for dinner.

I'd pass his room at various times of the day and discover him sitting at his makeshift desk, staring out the window. Various texts and ledgers lay open on the desk and on the bed behind him.

"What are you working on?" I inquired one afternoon.

As if awakened from a deep sleep, he turned around, startled. "What?"

"I'm sorry, Eli. I didn't mean to interrupt you."

I gently closed his door.

On the afternoon of a heavy snowfall, Eli stood in my studio doorway and announced that he was going to go out for a while.

He saw me gesturing toward the outside.

"You don't want me to drive the ragtop in a snowstorm?" he asked with an edge of defiance.

"Just be cautious," I said.

I could hear Mercy's tires spinning in the heavy drifts and watched it lurch down and away from our house.

For hours that long afternoon I fretted in the gradual darkening of the rooms. When dusk fully overtook the interior of our residence, I felt compelled to return to Eli's room to learn what he'd been working on so feverishly.

I turned on his desk lamp and saw opened the *Moby-Dick* text, the very one he'd brought with him from the start that he claimed Ishmael tutored him in. Like a devout worshiper with his Bible, he'd underlined countless passages throughout the manuscript.

He's regressing, I mused.

Too anxious to eat, I sat waiting up for him until after midnight, when I climbed into bed. Of course, I was unable to fall asleep and at some hour prior to daybreak I saw Mercy's yellow headlights glare over the snowy drifts in our driveway. Eli gunned the motor and snaked his way slowly up toward the house.

It was the first time in hours I experienced a sense of paradoxical joy.

Christ, what we can be thankful for, I thought.

He had returned, when I'd been prepared for something much worse.

There were two man-ghosts in the rooms that long day. The young man's and my very own.

Jeremiah had abandoned Mercy along a roadside when he caught on fire.

Eli had motored her home.

I lay listening to him climb the stairs on the way to his room.

Instead, there was a knock at my door.

"What is it?"

"Can I sleep with you tonight?"

I climbed out of bed. Eli looked as if he'd been walking all afternoon in the blizzard instead of riding in a car with a flimsy heater. He had never taken off his boots or his old Mackinaw, and his hair was glistening wet as if the snow on it had just melted. He appeared distraught . . . and mute.

I sat him down and began removing his clothes.

Fetching a flannel robe from my closet, I swaddled him in it and assisted him under the covers.

We lay quietly alongside each other in our separate beds for long minutes.

I finally broke the silence.

"Where did you go, Son?"

He didn't reply.

I feared that if I glanced out the window, I'd recognize another inside Mercy, awaiting Eli's return.

* * *

The next day at dusk, Eli went off on foot, never even bothering to turn over the car's ignition in the snowbound driveway. I followed him at a distance, for I had a premonition of where he had been the day before.

Despite the heavy precipitation that would have prevented skating, I believed he had gone seeking out the young woman in the red kerchief at the ice pond. He'd begun obsessing over the hours he'd spent enthralled by her company that one night, twirling her about the ice that mirrored a full moon, one hand gripping her knit headscarf with her clutching its other end, each laughing with un-bridled joy.

She wouldn't be there. But why would that concern him?

All that mattered was the narrative he had composed in his head. The one prompted by her breath enveloped in blue condensation and scented ice-crystal hair.

That way nothing died.

At some distance I knelt and witnessed Eli staring down at the darkened pond . . . and imagined what he saw. It was Alma pirouetting alone at its center, winding then unwinding her body in the red kerchief.

"She looked lovely, Eli."

He didn't answer as we followed our snow tracks back.

Moments later he stopped and turned to me.

"Alma never called while I was gone?"

"No."

He shook his head as if he should never had inquired.

"Of course not," he said. "It's why you've lived alone all these years. Isn't it?"

"Reluctantly."

Our unsweetened laughter echoed the void shadowing us this night back from Miller's Pond.

* * *

"*The ambiguous relationship between the fragments of our lives and their assemblage compose our stories.*"

That is what ran through my mind after Eli and I retired.

I worried for Eli's return to Naumkeag. Why was he back sharing my bedroom if not to regress to that place that had initially given his questing mind respite?

Once again, I envisioned Starbuck igniting the lamp and handing it to Queequeg:

I had failed the young man. But perhaps in that admission coils a lie.

Maybe it was he who had failed my urging to reunite with Jeremiah.

And now I had to prepare for his departure—once again.

Perhaps it is the losses we sustain, real or imagined, that give us reason to believe that our lives have substance.

Foolish Pride of Reason
Seldom have I known any profound being that had anything to say to this world, unless forced to stammer out something by way of getting a living. Oh! happy that the world is such an excellent listener.[xxiv]

* * *

Outside, Mercy encrusted by snow became the metaphor for his impending departure.

I found myself mindlessly playing Charon's tunes on the upright that was really Eli's. I'd tell stories that veiled no meaning to what our current situation portended.

It was painfully apparent that he was also anxious.

Or was it something else?

I kept rehearsing the image of him whipping Alma about the pond's caution edges.

But here in our fallow quarters, it was the two of us tied together by some enigmatic bond, navigating each day's light hours before the blessed escape of sleep . . . but not laughing.

Holding on, fearful of losing our grip to the other.

Yet we still shared a bedroom. It was Eli's wish.

Just as Jeremiah as a child had slipped into bed with me.

It was our sanctuary.

Days transpired as if the ice would never begin to crack and slowly melt back into water.

How long could this go on?

The snow continued to accumulate on Mercy, an amorphous mound now, and only the pair of us knew what lay under.

Then it occurred.

Eli stood by my bedside one night shaking me awake.

He was possessed by fear.

"She's calling me home."

"What do you mean?" I sat up and pulled him alongside me in bed. His body pulsed as if he was overcome by an extreme draft. I embraced him, attempting to quell his shivering.

"You must get a hold of yourself, Eli. It's just a dream."

He shook his head. "No. It's for real.

"I have not told you, but she has appeared before me dancing in that empty dining hall with those sable-coated men. She is bedecked in red and her hair is down. Charon is at the keyboard. As alive as you are right this moment. So close I could reach out and touch her garment. The perfume she wore when she went out at night in my youth. How could I forget it? When she left me alone, I cried, because that heady fragrance lingered in the room as if she were still present. Except I knew it was going to invade the nostrils of some stranger.

"Well, there are no other men in her life now. She wants me back. I must go."

Eli stood up next to my bed and let out a cry as if he'd been drawn out of his body by a whale line.

"*Oh, the fucking irony of it all!*" he keened.

"Eli, stop!" I cried.

He turned at the doorway and dispassionately stared at me. "Why, because it makes no sense?

"That I'm returning from whence I came because it makes no sense? That's why it is so fucking real, John Proctor.

"It's what we don't understand that beguiles us. And why am I going? Because all my other fathers are dead. None of them were good enough for her to call on in this moment, this last fucking dance.

"And if Charon isn't available? I'll sing.

"Does that make sense to you?"

Eli went into his room to pack.

* * *

The days and weeks following his departure evaporated like I was in a trance. Deep snowdrifts gathered about the house, unmarred by footprints. I neither wrote nor painted and rarely ate.

Eli had closed the door to his room. I never opened it.

There were hallucinatory moments when I imagined him inside there. Some nights as I lay in bed, I'd hear him quoting passages of his Naumkeag authors. One of those times, I listened in on a discussion between him and Queequeg. It unsettled me because when Queequeg laughed, it sounded like Jeremiah. Then I wondered if all three were in that room.

It wasn't until the first week in March when the drifts began to melt that Mercy reappeared. Perhaps seeing her emerge outside my window each day gradually reintroduced me to reality. Once the muddy driveway surfaced, I made my first venture outside to purchase some staples. The proprietor of the grocery store down the road never mentioned my absence. His "good morning" was as hearty and genuine as I recalled.

Returning to the house, I hesitated prior to entering, debating if I wanted to look inside Mercy in the chance that I might find some remnant of Eli.

Unable to resist the notion, I opened the driver's side door. There on its green Naugahyde seat was an envelope in his handwriting addressed to me.

I was afraid to touch it for fear all the pain would return.

Then what?

I dared not reflect.

Taking my place at the kitchen table where Eli and I shared most of our meals, I opened the envelope and read:

Dear John Proctor,

I left this note to you inside Mercy because there was something I never told you. You recall that trip she and I took across the States? Well, Jeremiah sat right alongside me. We laughed and exchanged stories just like you and I did. I took the liberty one night when we were driving through a long stretch of Iowa to ask about his running across the wheat field all aflame. Telling him I couldn't get the image out of my head. Was it for real? At first, he didn't want to talk about it. But after lighting a cigarette that we shared, he opened up, saying it was the damndest thing he'd ever done.

"Honest to Christ, Eli, I felt somehow redeemed. Making myself into something I could never become in a hundred years. Me flying across that field waving my arms, surer than hell the flames reaching to the sky would carry me with them. That was the image in my head. Like one of those mythology tales, you know. Jeremiah Proctor lifting off this fallow earth, the days, months, and years of too damn little taking place. The hurts and disappointments. And even when something kind of good occurs, it just wouldn't last. In the meantime, I'm getting older ... meaning dying, 'cause that's the truth. Each damn year I was moving closer to the old boneyard. That's what I was seein' my life and everybody else's being. We're all two-stepping to marble town. Why not just take up residence there?"

And Jeremiah is laughing and smacking his thigh while he's telling me all this. I loved him more than ever, your brother, I did.

"That's why I lit myself and went up to the sky in flames, Eli. The most courageous and honest thing I'd ever done in life. Most truthful, too. Wouldn't you say?"

He saved me, John.

Jeremiah saved me. When we were returning home and traveling through Pittsburgh long after midnight, I had the urge to drive off one of its many bridges straight into the Allegheny River. Thinking I'd seen enough. I'd recognized yours and my time together was destined to end. That I'd have to return to Naumkeag ... and I now knew what that meant.

Jeremiah had dozed off. What better time than now, I thought, and began flooring Mercy, knowing I'd break through the bridge's parapets.

When I felt Jeremiah grab the wheel and pedal the brakes hard.

"What in Christname are you doing?" he yelled. "Whose car do you think this is?"

"Yours," I said.

"Fucking right," he answered. "It's my story too, Son. Not yours."

I just wanted to share this with you.

Love,

Eli

EPILOGUE

In his absence, I began to view my time with Eli as a novel that I had once written and, with trepidation, loved. Over time, however, I was only able to recall the narrative's highlights while its storyline faded off into a distant memory.

I returned to the life I had led prior to the young man's appearance, while the hours I spent at the easel attenuated. A goodly portion of my workday occurred on my studio couch where I'd gaze at the ceiling and witness snippets of my years give performances in miniature. Most were pleasant. Some less so.

Then when the half light of the day bled across its walls, I'd enter the kitchen to prepare dinner. Bedtime happened early, often before nightfall.

Even when old friends reached out to me, I responded cordially but little more. Neither did I answer the phone nor reply to left messages. Only rarely.

My diet of dreams and dwindling memories afforded me a dispassionate existence uninterrupted by surprises.

Two years following Eli's departure, a septuagenarian gentleman appeared at my door one July day. He claimed to have long admired my antique automobile, and would I be interested in selling it, given that it had sat idle for years there in the driveway. The man said he was retired and spent his free time refurbishing the older models and was especially attracted to the Plymouth ragtop because of its rumble seat.

Mercy being gone could only help hasten the healing process of my and Eli's time together, so the ragtop was hoisted onto a trailer bed and taken away.

Within hours of that event I'd rid every vestige of him from the guestroom. Now only the waning memory of the young man remained.

One very cold and overcast November afternoon several years later, I was resting in my living room, preoccupied by the distinct chill in the air. It felt as if the wind had shot through my modest brick home. *Would there be any place in the house to get warm*? I wondered. And was just about to get up and build a fire in the hearth, when I was startled by a bundled-up male loudly tapping on the window.

Was I imagining it?

The tapping was incessant, accompanied by a gloved hand waving.

I warily strode to the glass pane, and within inches of my face was that of my brother, whose ironic expression registered: *Why are you surprised?*

He kept pointing to the door for me to open it.

I fell back onto the sofa, sitting there in a daze and suspended fright.

What's got into me?

Shaking my head as if to erase his image, I once again glanced back at the window. Jeremiah patiently awaited my resolve as I, in turn, began igniting the room's lamps and overhead lights. Now the knocking was at the front door.

I could hear my name called out again and again.

It was only when I heard the word "Eli" did I began to gather my senses about me. *"Eli?"* I said to myself. *"But you conspicuously aren't!"*

I peered out the narrow window at the door's apex. Jeremiah's face on its other side. He cried, "John Proctor. It's me, Eli!"

When I opened it, the two of us stood inches apart like strangers struggling to stitch their memories of each other rapidly together so that words might form.

It was Eli who first grinned widely and embraced me. "Oh, John, I've missed you so."

I stiffened under his grip. I hadn't wanted to hear these words for fear that all the reserves I'd built up over his absence would fail and I'd begin quaking.

He placed his hands on my shoulders and held me at arm's length.

"What is it, dear friend? I thought you'd be overjoyed to see me again."

With difficulty, I nodded then uttered a greeting.

"Welcome back, Jeremiah."

At which point Eli began to laugh uproariously. He led me to an overstuffed chair and pulled a side chair close to him. Each of us sat there mutely bathing in the shadowy moment.

"Yes, my mother has said the same. 'You're his spitting image,' she claims. And now you have confirmed it."

He placed his hands on my knees.

"I've a friend in the car so I can't stay, but I want to return in the morning so we can spend some quality time together. There is so much I must tell you. I just had to come back to see you, to be with you again, John. You gave me life. And look at me. It's working!"

Eli stood up and left me sitting there. At the door he turned to say he'd bring breakfast for us in the morning.

"My friend and I will eat at the hotel downtown, then turn in. It's been a long drive."

Watching Eli climb into Mercy's driver's seat, I caught a glimpse of the man sitting alongside.

I had sold him the car years earlier.

And seeing their faces together as they backed out of the driveway, I was certain it was Ishmael.

Following their departure, I again experienced an overwhelming premonition that Eli was returning to the ice pond and that I must follow him. It had turned dark and was snowing heavily. Upon arriving, I spotted Ishmael in black garb standing alongside Mercy, parked at the pond's edge with its headlights illuminating the ice. Eli was in skates at its center, circling, vortex-like. Lost in his own space.

An exorcism, I thought.

Suddenly from out of the woods surrounding the pond a man in a white suit appeared who strode out onto the ice within a body length of Eli and spoke.

"What are you doing here, Son?"

It was Jeremiah's ghost.

Eli ceased skating and stepped toward the figure.

"I've come home, Father."

Reaching out to embrace him, I witnessed my brother's suit legs burst into flames . . . yet Jeremiah remained unperturbed, at consummate peace.

"I'll remember," he says, caressing Eli's face and hair.

But then pleaded, *"Let me go, Son. It's our story . . ."* before withdrawing into the shadowy fringe where the other MacLeish Sq. denizens—Eli's mother in red, Cotton Mather with his coterie, and Charon—looked on.

Eli never showed the next morning.

Nor did I ever hear from him again.

I chose to let it go, believing the visitation was also a message from my brother to me. Years passed without incident. I found that I had begun physically aging at an accelerated pace. Mentally, I believed I was still of sound mind. But who was to know for certain since I kept my own company?

One autumn day I was wandering through the fields surrounding my property when I felt the urge to continue down a path that led to the pond where I last saw Eli. I was merely curious as to what changes nature had made over the years. I knew from local folk that skating had ceased there over two decades ago. I hadn't realized it had been that long, having lost all sense of time. My body knew.

When I arrived at what I believed was the site, I noted that the pond had disappeared. It was an overgrown field with maple, oak, hawthorn, and ash saplings. I spotted what appeared to be portions of a stone foundation from the old skating shed. Venturing farther into the field, I came upon the rusted-out remnants of Mercy.

One of its doors hung open. The driver's side one was missing. There was a slight breeze that day and the door moved . . . a scraping sound like a rodent's cry. The ragtop of course had rotted away. The rumble seat lay open to a rusted-out cavity. Scavengers, I presumed, had removed its wheels. Bittersweet had grown up through the floorboards, encircling the stick shift and rising to drape the rearview mirror like a purloined garter with a tendril of red berries.

Mercy wasn't Queequeg's life-buoy as Eli might have wished, but he'd conspicuously left it there for his father.

It was only then—as I ventured deeper into the woods—that

I knew this was surely where my brother ran that day—years earlier—on fire and fanning the wind.

ENDNOTES:

i *INFERNO*, Canto XXXIV, pp 391

ii *MOBY-DICK*, A Norton Critical Edition, 2nd Edition, Ch. 110, pp 364

iii Ibid Ch. 10, pp 55

iv Ibid Ch. 42, pp 162

v Ibid Ch. 48, pp 187

vi Ibid Ch. 93, pp 322

vii Ibid Ch. 6, pp 43

viii *NATHANIEL HAWTHORNE*, Collected Novels, *The Scarlet Letter*, Ch. 4, pp 181

ix Ibid Ch. 18, pp 290

x *INFERNO*, A New Verse Translation by Michael Palma, Canto XXXII, pp 359

xi *MOBY-DICK*, A Norton Critical Edition, 2nd Edition, Ch. 28, pp 109

xii Ibid Ch. 58, pp 225

xiii Ibid Ch. 48, pp 187

xiv Ibid Ch. 42, pp 162

xv Ibid Ch. 102, pp 345

xvi Ibid Ch. 10, pp 56

xvii *NATHANIEL HAWTHORNE*, Collected Novels, *The Scarlet Letter,* Ch. 16, pp 277

xviii Ibid *The Custom House, Introductory,* pp 126

xix Ibid Ch. 13, pp 258

xx Ibid Ch. 16, pp 277

xxi *MOBY-DICK*, A Norton Critical Edition, 2nd Edition, Epilogue, pp 427

xxii FERNANDO PESSOA, *A Little Larger Than the Entire Universe, Selected Poems,* pp 133

xxiii *MOBY-DICK*, A Norton Critical Edition, 2nd Edition, Ch. 110, pp 365

xxiv Ibid Ch. 85, pp 291

AFTERWORD

Edward Said wrote about Beethoven's late style. He wrote of late style as that time wherein the artist, freed from the expected cultural and historical restraints of form and content, unleashes a newness that both confounds and instructs. Dennis Must has achieved that hour of newness in *MacLeish Sq.* With its visual complexities coupled to broad-ranging literary interconnections, Must raises the text to a "beyond" state where the reader has to let go of what they know. The reader must accept that their own hidden story has been eclipsed and take this writing on its own without any preconceived notions of what "a novel" is or should be. Roland Barthes, now out of fashion to the post-postmodern mind, wrote in his essays—*Le degré zéro de l'écriture*—that there are two kinds of writers, which he called *l'écrivain* and *l'écrivant*. Must, in *MacLeish Sq.* brings us a third iteration of writer as his work approaches mythic status in which time, character, past, present, alive, dead—just a few of the literary polarities inhabiting this writing—interact at a level no reader can accept without relinquishing his or her own sense of person and being. Interweaving Dante, Melville, Hawthorne, and Pirandello into a single narrative that seizes the essence of each isn't a style most readers will be comfortable with. Here, however, Must puts them together with such skill that the author lives on par with the masters. It will take an honest reader to admit—I have never read anything like this.

And this is why: Must gives us a writing that isn't built on the usual dramatic structure with its twists and disguises, its dramatic plot points and ridiculous and predictable revelations, but a study in both style and structure that foregoes the ordinary and launches the reader on an experience perhaps unique in American writing. I have nothing but admiration for the chosen format in this writing although, as a novelist, I know that Must will run headlong into a cultural buzzsaw when this piece meets the mechanical mind where the puzzle presented by the short line sections enclosing long-arcing philosophical aspects will bring the reader to a meaningful crossroads and a profound intellectual challenge. This writing is a form that generates its own dynamics. The artist here takes chances in structure while maintaining an absolute connection to the canonical language and in doing so produces in his late style a shining delicacy in a world that exists beyond its artistic past. Taken on its own and as it is, this writing brings rich rewards to the daring reader bored with living on the flat plain of latter-day American novels.

—Jack Remick, author of *Gabriella and The Widow*, *The California Quartet*, *Blood*, and numerous other works

BIOGRAPHICAL NOTE

Dennis Must is the author of three novels: *Brother Carnival* (Red Hen Press 2018), *Hush Now, Don't Explain* (Coffeetown Press 2014), and *The World's Smallest Bible* (Red Hen Press 2014); as well as three short story collections: *Going Dark* (Coffeetown Press 2016), *Oh, Don't Ask Why* (Red Hen Press 2007), and *Banjo Grease* (Creative Arts Book Company 2000 and Red Hen Press 2019). He won the 2014 Dactyl Foundation Literary Fiction Award for *Hush Now, Don't Explain*; in addition, he was a finalist in the 2019 Next Generation Indie Book Awards for *Banjo Grease*, the 2016 International Book Awards for *Going Dark*, and the 2014 USA Best Book Award in Literary Fiction for *The World's Smallest Bible*, the 2008 Michigan Literary Fiction Award Finalist, University of Michigan Press, and the 2009 Faulkner Society's William Faulkner-Wm. Wisdom Creative Writing Novel Competition Finalist. A member of the Authors Guild, his plays have been produced off-off-Broadway. He resides with his wife in Salem, Massachusetts.

CPSIA information can be obtained
at www.ICGtesting.com
Printed in the USA
LVHW051352161022
730743LV00004B/8